Roshmila Bhattacharya is a senior journalist who, in a career spanning over three decades, has worked with *Filmfare*, *The Asian Age*, *Indian Express*, *Hindustan Times* and *The Times of India*. She also brainstormed with the late National Award-winning editor, Rauf Ahmed, on a monthly film magazine, *Zee Premiere*. She has contributed to *The Telegraph*, *National Herald*, *Deccan Herald*, *Free Press Journal* and *Rediff.Com*, breaking several stories on the national platform, was a columnist for over 15 years and continues to find enjoyment in the field of entertainment journalism.

In July 2019, she released her first book, *Bad Man*, a biography of Gulshan Grover, published by Penguin. Her second book, *Matinee Men: A Journey Through Bollywood*, was published by Rupa Publications in December 2019. It is listed amongst the 20 Best Bollywood Movie e-books of All Time by Book Authority, and *The Times of India* recommended it as one of the eight books every Bollywood lover should read.

In July 2022, *Tera Chhalaava*, a crime anthology for which she has written four stories, released on Hungama Play and MX Player.

SPOOKED!

Bollywood's Encounters with the Paranormal

Roshmila Bhattacharya

Om Books International

First published in 2024 by

Om Books International

Corporate & Editorial Office
A-12, Sector 64, Noida 201 301
Uttar Pradesh, India
Phone: +91 120 477 4100
Email: editorial@ombooks.com
Website: www.ombooksinternational.com

Sales Office
107, Ansari Road, Darya Ganj,
New Delhi 110 002, India
Phone: +91 11 4000 9000
Email: sales@ombooks.com
Website: www.ombooks.com

ISBN: 978-81-960433-2-2

Printed in India

10 9 8 7 6 5 4 3 2 1

To my parents, Deepali and Manas,
who are still with me in spirit…

Contents

PREFACE

The Lady Vanished

You often hear about people disappearing, but it's hard to imagine it happening in your own family. Unfortunately, it did happen in mine.

My grandfather's aunt lived with her sons in a house that was always bustling with people. It was just another day; she went about her usual chores and in the evening, a friend dropped by. When her friend was leaving, she insisted on seeing her off. The cook in the kitchen saw the two elderly women walk out, chatting.

It was a little past 7 p.m. and there was a nip in the air. Involuntarily, my grandfather's aunt shivered, wishing she had worn her slippers and a shawl. Her friend admonished her, telling her that she would catch a cold and urged her to go back inside. But she insisted on waiting by the main door till her friend had reached the end of the lane. Her friend hurried away, looking over her shoulder before she took a turn. That was the last time anyone ever saw my grandfather's aunt.

When the family realized she was not around, they went looking for her everywhere. But they couldn't find her.

A few months after the incident, I heard my mother discussing it and the story fired my imagination. An avid

Sherlock Holmes, Byomkesh Bakshi and Agatha Christie fan, I wondered where the elderly woman could have vanished.

Did she leave the house without telling anyone? If so, why? How far could she have gone on a cold evening without her slippers or woollens? Was she headed home or did she take a detour to the market to buy something? Her friend didn't remember her saying she wanted anything and she wasn't carrying a purse. How far could she have gone without someone noticing her? Even if she had suddenly fallen ill or suffered a temporary bout of amnesia, a neighbour would have come to her aid or alerted her sons. Where was she? What had become of her? Was she still alive? These questions, and some more, came to mind. They remained unanswered.

The family refused to give up on her. As days turned to weeks and months to years, the search broadened—from the neighbourhood to the city, from across the state to the country. The cops had been intimated, her photograph had been circulated, and news of her disappearance had reached far and wide. Whenever her sons received any news about someone resembling her from any part of the country, they would rush there with renewed hope, only to return home disappointed.

After a while, they started making peace with the idea that their mother was no longer alive. Maybe she had been in an accident? Or maybe she had run into someone who had killed her? It couldn't have been for ransom because there had never been a demand for money. 'If only somebody would tell her sons that she is dead, they might find some peace of mind,' I heard my grandmother tell my mother. And somebody did.

Before we go any further, let me tell you a bit about my grandparents. My grandfather, Rabindranath Bannerjee, had worked for the Darbhanga Raj. He and my *nani* (grandmother), Mira, lived in the fifth largest city of Bihar, in a huge bungalow with a wraparound veranda, which gave access to some of the rooms from outside if the doors were unlatched.

A cobbled path from the main gate led up the driveway to the porch. Three stairs up from there and you came to a smaller gate which you had to unlatch to get to the veranda. While this gate was never locked, it was always kept latched because my grandparents did not want Pigu, their Pomeranian, wandering around the property, which was pretty large, with a garden and a field in the front. Beyond the field was a stream where my grandfather, my mother and her cousins would sometimes go fishing. And while there were lots of people around during the day, once the sun went down, it was just the two of them.

Late one night, my grandmother woke up to the sound of the main gate opening with a creak. She heard someone walk up the path and wondered why the dog wasn't barking. She could hear the person stop just below the smaller gate. As nani listened with bated breath, she heard the latch being lifted. The gate opened and the visitor was on the veranda. Nani was expecting to hear a knock on the door or the doorbell, but the person continued along the veranda and walked to the rear side of the house.

All the windows to the rooms facing the front were shuttered and the doors locked from inside. But to nani's surprise, after a while she heard the person prowling inside their storeroom. After debating on whether to wake up my grandfather, she decided against it. It would be foolish for an elderly man to confront a thief, who might be carrying a weapon, she thought. She told herself that at the most, they would lose a few sacks of rice. There was nothing valuable in the room, thankfully.

Her ears were focused on what was happening in the room. After a while, she heard the person leave the room, even though she didn't hear any doors opening or closing. Some time later, the small gate opened with a gentle creak and their mysterious visitor went down the steps and headed towards the main gate. 'Don't ask me why, but in that instant, I just knew that it was a woman, and she was barefoot,' nani told us much later.

She couldn't sleep after the incident and at dawn, the moment she could see daylight, she ran to the storeroom to check what had been stolen. She found that nothing had been touched or moved. Yet Pigu, who had been unnaturally silent the previous night when the person had broken in, was now spinning around the room, barking furiously.

Mystified, nani narrated the incident to my grandfather, who confessed that he had consulted a clairvoyant about his aunt. The man had asked for an item of clothing she used to wear, so he had got one of her sons to send across a sari. The psychic had chanted a mantra and told him to keep the sari in a room that was not used much. 'I left the sari in the storeroom at the back,' he confirmed.

My grandmother admonished him for keeping her in the dark and insisted that he share the incident with the psychic. When he did, my grandfather was told that his aunt was definitely dead, though the psychic had no idea how it had happened. What he did know was that her spirit was restless. He urged my grandfather to tell her sons to stop searching for her and perform her last rites, so she would be at peace.

The story doesn't end there. I still have to tell you about my grandmother's recurring dream. In her dream, my grandfather's aunt, who had actually been only a few years older than nani, appeared and told her, 'Mira, I am craving your chum chums (a Bengali sweet), will you make some for me?'

This particular *mithai* (sweet) had been one of nani's specialties and everyone's favourite. Initially, she ignored the dream. But when the same dream recurred three nights in a row, with my grandfather's aunt literally pleading for the sweets, saying she was ravenous, nani woke up early the next day and started preparing the chum chums. After my grandfather had finished his morning cuppa, she laid the sweets out on a banana leaf and instructed him to leave them on the bank of the stream, under a tree.

He did, reporting that there was no one there at that hour, apart from the birds and a few strays. 'I won't be surprised if they eat the sweets,' he scoffed. Nani pretended she hadn't heard him.

To my grandfather's surprise, when he went down around noon, he found that the sweets were lying there untouched, even though the workers were in the field by then and their children were playing around. He went back a couple of times throughout the day, the chum chums remained untouched. It was only at night, after everyone returned to their homes, that they disappeared. The next morning, he saw the empty banana leaf exactly where he had left it.

My grandmother told me these stories when I visited her during the holidays. My eyes flitted around the large kitchen apprehensively, as I asked her if the ghost was still around and if she had seen her. Nani shook her head, 'No, I haven't, but I feel her presence.' My eyes grew wider, 'You mean she is here now?' My grandmother laughed, 'Not now, but when I am alone in the house, I sense her presence at times. The dog used to bark earlier, but now even Pigu seems to have accepted her. She is family after all.'

I still remember my grandmother's calm, matter-of-fact tone when she was telling me this, prompting me to ask, 'But aren't you scared nani?' She shook her head, 'Why should I be scared? I know she will never harm us. And to be honest, it used to get quite lonely, being alone in this huge house all day. I enjoy the company.'

Was my nani psychic? A medium? No, she was just an ordinary woman who had had only this one brush with a supposed spirit. Thankfully, she was completely unruffled.

I have never had any paranormal experience, but I learnt early on not to doubt the existence of spirits. I believe they are around us, in a parallel world, but if they are one of your own, it is best to let them coexist. As my nani had asserted years ago, they mean no harm.

But when it's black magic, there's need to be worried, very worried. Until I was ten, I lived in Shillong for five years. We stayed in the Meghalayan capital in a quaint cottage elevated by bamboo poles. Life was idyllic. I ran from one friend's house to the next and plucked fruits from the orchards in the neighbourhood.

Apart from a few months, our stay there was a lot of fun. There was this period when my mother refused to let me go for birthday parties or play dates after rumours of *jaadu tona* (black magic) started circulating. It was said that some of the local families kept snakes that they worshipped in their ancestral homes. According to their belief, the snake god demanded a human sacrifice once a year. Since they could not openly sacrifice humans, these families used black magic to appease the deity.

Friends and neighbours would be invited home and without them being aware, a few strands of hair and a bit of their clothing would be stealthily snipped off while their attention was diverted. These offerings were placed in the sanctum sanctorum. As days passed into weeks, the 'victim' would fall ill, grow weak and become deathly pale, as if blood was being drained out of the body. Doctors, mystified by this strange illness, would not be able to offer any cure and eventually, the person would die.

'It's the snake sucking out their life force,' was the dire prediction of the wise and the elderly. I was too young to worry about life and death and the grey areas in between. But I remember the anxious frown my mother perpetually wore at the time, as I pestered her for not being allowed to run free.

Even after we left the hills and moved to the plains, maa would start her *jhad phuk* (exorcism) on me if I fell ill too frequently. When I returned home after playing with my friends, I would find her roasting a handful of dried red chillies on the gas stove. Once the chillies turned brown, she would call out to me. As I stood in front of her, she would mutter a mantra and wave the chillies around me, throwing them over her shoulder. She didn't look back and I was warned to avert my eyes too.

I don't know if this ritual worked, but I remember that the typical pungent odour of roasted chillies, which usually triggers a coughing fit and causes eyes to water, was sometimes absent during these occasions. When I had asked maa about this years later, when she was performing the same ritual on my daughter, Ranjika, she explained that if there was no smell, it meant someone had put a hex on you and the chillies had drawn it away.

Have I ever performed this ritual? Never. But something strange did happen to me at the time of my daughter's birth. It had been a difficult pregnancy because just a year-and-a-half before Ranjika was born, I had lost a foetus owing to undetected fibroids in my uterus. Subsequently, I had to undergo a surgery and five benign tumours were removed from the uterus. It was a complicated surgery and I knew my chances of conceiving again were slim, so I was delighted when I was pregnant again. The doctor was wary, putting me under house arrest after the second trimester. As soon as I completed eight months, I was advised to have the baby via C-section, even if the baby was born three weeks premature.

I chose 6 March as the day of the operation, because it was a Saturday and my husband would have the weekend off. I wanted our baby to be the first delivery of the day, so I was wheeled into the Operation Theatre around 8.30 a.m. and administered a shot. That was when I realized that anaesthesia doesn't work on me. The injection numbed all sensation from waist down, but I did not go under as expected. I was fully conscious and aware of everything happening around me, despite a second jab in the spine.

I knew exactly when the doctor used his scalpel, even though I didn't feel any pain. I heard him discussing my case and the nurse warning him that my blood pressure had dropped alarmingly. I heard someone shout, 'It's a girl!' I had been waiting impatiently to welcome my miracle baby into the world. After learning that I had a daughter, I heaved a sigh of relief. And let go.

'She's slipping away,' I heard the nurse say, as I went rushing down a dark tunnel. I was completely at peace, as I moved towards the promised light. Then, I heard someone say, 'The baby's not crying.' This was followed by the sound of gentle slaps to elicit a response from my unresponsive child. The weight of motherhood settled heavily around my tired shoulders, interrupting my flight. I turned back, re-entered the room and approached my daughter. Almost instantly, I heard a hearty wail. As I smiled, I heard someone say, 'The mother is fine too; the crisis has passed.' My daughter is twenty-four today, and I am eternally grateful that I could spend all these years with her.

In addition to being a mother, I am also a film journalist. In the course of many interviews, I had heard actors, directors and film technicians talk about that 'terrifying experience' or the 'gift'. That's what prompted me to write this book.

While horror is not as popular a genre in Hindi cinema as action, romance or even comedy, at least a dozen scary stories, if not more, are brought to the screen every year. Occasionally, one of them turns out to be a surprise hit. The Ramsays minted money with *Do Gaz Zameen Ke Neeche* (1972), *Purana Mandir* (1984) and *Veerana* (1988), while Raj Kumar Kohli made blockbusters like *Nagin* (1976) and *Jaani Dushman* (1979). Films like *Mahal* (1949), *Madhumati* (1958) and *Woh Kaun Thi?* (1964) became cult classics, but largely, horror remained B-grade entertainment.

It was Ram Gopal Verma with *Raat* (1992), *Bhoot* (2003), *Phoonk* (2008), along with anthologies like *Darna Mana Hai* (2003) and *Darna Zaroori Hai* (2006), and Vikram Bhatt with *Raaz* (2002), *1920* (2008) and *Haunted-3D* (2011), who reinvented the genre. They brought the supernatural to the multiplexes and attracted a more elite audience to sample their fares. Ekta Kapoor carried the trend forward with *Ragini MMS* and its sequel (2011, 2014) and now, even a Karan Johar is sailing the seas with *Bhoot Part One: The Haunted Ship* (2020), while Akshay Kumar drapes himself in a sari to play a transgender ghost in *Laxmii* (2020), Ronnie Screwvala and Ashi Dua produce a *Ghost Stories* (2020) anthology for Netflix and Dinesh Vijan creates a horror universe with *Stree* (2018), its upcoming sequel, *Roohi* (2021) and *Bhediya* (2022).

I've been a die-hard (no pun intended) horror buff since I can remember, lapping up all these films, and some more. In my teens, I would frequent the neighbourhood video-cassette library and happily carry home a *Dak Bangla* (1987) or a *Bandh Darwaza* (1990), much to the exasperation of my parents. The next day, when I returned the VCD (later DVD), the amused shop owner would ask me how many times I had screamed out loud. I would tell him with a patronizing smile that the film had only managed to evoke some titters from me. Soon, it became a game between us to see which *bhootiya kahani* (ghost story) could give me the jitters. Few actually did, but in the process of watching them, my appetite for horror grew. Soon, I was asking myself if what I was seeing on screen ever happened in real life. Did the actors in these films experience some paranormal activity while shooting for them? Did their makers have any anecdotes that could chill me to the bone the way their movies had never done? For that matter, did anyone in the film fraternity have any real-life ghost story to narrate? During the Covid-19 pandemic, I started making calls.

Some individuals, who had previously confided in me about their eerie experiences, suddenly changed their tune when I mentioned my intention to document their encounters in a book. They denied ever experiencing anything unusual and claimed that such events had never happened to them.

Some people wondered if I had suddenly gone crazy and stopped responding to my texts or calls.

A few, however, opened up and shared their experiences—ones that had spooked them, left them confused and in some instances, even altered the trajectory of their lives. I'm immensely grateful to them for placing their trust in me because it's solely due to their willingness to share their stories that this book has become a reality. If you're ready for some genuine paranormal encounters, read on...

1

JUHI CHAWLA

It's Hard to Say Goodbye...

She was in the seventh standard in school when she landed an assignment which required her to write what she wanted to be when she grew up. While her classmates went with tried-and-tested choices like doctor, teacher and artist, Juhi Chawla surprised everyone, including herself, by stating that she wanted to be 'rich and famous'.

'I wasn't the prettiest girl in class or even the smartest. I was just a regular kid from a decent background in an all-girls' convent school who happened to see a film titled *Rich and Famous* (1981), revolving around two successful but very different writers, whose friendship spans a quarter of a century. Perhaps that's how the words had crept into my essay and they made my friends laugh,' reminisces Juhi, who despite the sniggering giggles, continued to cling on to the 'dream'. 'Only as I grew older, I added two more words—happy and healthy—to the rich and famous,' she shares, pointing out that she figured it would be no fun being rich and famous if one was miserable or unwell.

In 1984, Juhi took part in the Femina Miss India beauty contest because some of her friends had filled the form too.

'And if they could do it, so could I,' she reasons, admitting that never even in her wildest dreams had she imagined that she would walk away with the crown.

A few months later, she landed a break in the Bollywood biggie, *Sultanat* (1986), followed by the blockbuster *Qayamat Se Qayamat Tak* (1988). Over the next three decades, with several hits, and some misses, Juhi Chawla went on to become not just happy and healthy, but a rich and famous actress too. 'Be careful what you wish for; the universe may conspire to make it happen,' she laughs.

However, along with a dream come true came the nightmares. They started around the same time, when Juhi was ten or eleven years old. 'I loved my mother a lot. Some nights I would have nightmares, and in the nightmares, I watched her die. It was never any other member of the family, only her. She would fall from a tall building or perish in a fire and I would wake up terrified, bathed in cold sweat, only reassured when I saw that my mother was safe and fine,' Juhi recounts.

In 1998, Mona Chawla accompanied her daughter to Prague, for the shooting of *Duplicate* (1998). The day after they arrived, she went out for her usual early-morning walk and was fatally knocked down in a hit-and-run accident on the street of the Czech capital. 'I was completely shattered, it was my first encounter with death, and that too, losing the one person who meant the world to me. I felt the ground slipping from under my feet. I could only hope that when I woke up, it would turn out to be another sad and painful dream,' Juhi reminisces.

However, this time, it was for real. 'When I was in hospital, looking down at the lifeless body of the person I had loved the most, I was shocked and speechless. But as I stood there, transfixed, I watched myself repeatedly tell her, "Maa, go in peace, I love you, Maa, go in peace..." It was an out-of-the-body experience and I could almost "see" the words coming, not from my mind or even my heart, but from somewhere far deeper, from my spirit to her soul. It was surreal!' Juhi recounts.

In retrospect, she believes the words came from the universe, to liberate the soul of her mother from the bondage of love that had kept her rooted to this world even after she was gone.

The same thing happened again, this time when she went to visit her much-loved aunt in her last moments, to spare her younger cousin the pain of loss. 'I found myself assuring my aunt who had just passed away that I would always be there for her daughter, perhaps giving her solace she so desperately needed to hear before going away forever,' Juhi muses.

In 2010, she had just landed in Mumbai, after an IPL match of her franchise, Kolkata Knight Riders, when the Jet Airways staff hurried across to convey an urgent message from her husband, industrialist Jay Mehta, that she should call him immediately. 'I had caught the 11 p.m. flight back with our two children (Jahnavi and Arjun) while Jay had stayed back in Kolkata. It was very late in the night, around 1.30 a.m., and I was worried as I made the call, wondering what could have happened that was so urgent,' she flashbacks to the moment.

Nothing in her life could have prepared her for what she heard next. Bobby Chawla, her only brother, had collapsed after suffering a brain haemorrhage. 'He was in ICU and needed immediate surgery. I was to go to the hospital immediately.'

Jay was out of town, so was Bobby's wife, Renu. Juhi sent her young children home, and with the responsibility of her brother's life resting on her shoulders, drove through the city, alone, to the hospital. 'It felt like a scene straight out of a scary medical drama. I was filled with dread as I drove through the dark, desolate streets, the hospital, looming in the distance,' she narrates.

When she finally reached the hospital, with its dimly lit, deserted corridors and cold, blue walls, Juhi discovered that they had already wheeled Bobby into the operation theatre. They were impatiently waiting for her to arrive to give the doctors permission to operate on him and stem the flow of blood in his brain. 'I couldn't see my brother who was somewhere beyond the glass doors of the OT. I had never faced this kind of situation before and could not comprehend what the doctors were saying. In a daze, I signed the papers for the surgery. The next day, Bobby went into a coma,' she informs.

It was disheartening, but the family and the doctors hoped that Bobby would recover. From his friends Juhi learnt that on the evening that he suffered the stroke, her brother, who was the CEO of Red Chillies Entertainment, had been somewhat stressed. He had let his chauffeur off early from duty and driven himself to a restaurant to meet some friends. He had arrived before them, and sitting at the table, was on a call on his cell phone, when he collapsed and fell to the floor.

By a stroke of luck, a person sitting at a nearby table recognized Bobby and rushed him to hospital. 'Once there, someone had thought of calling Farah Khan (director-choreographer) who immediately rushed to the hospital and signed the papers for him to be admitted. 'Had it not been for the prompt action of complete strangers, we might have lost Bobby in the restaurant itself. That made us believe that he had a chance, and we moved heaven and earth to get him the best medical assistance,' asserts Juhi.

The days that followed passed in a blur. Her brother was surrounded by beeping machines, needles were stuck into every part of his body and a ventilator was breathing for him. 'We consulted every doctor in the hospital, in the city, in the world. I was panic-stricken, remembering another nightmare from when I was a child. As I woke up from deep sleep, I would try to move my limbs, but my body would not oblige. Terrified, I would struggle in my sleep, try to scream for help, but there was no sound and no movement. I felt that I was trapped in my own body, till I broke out of the sleep paralysis and actually opened my eyes.' She shivers at the memory. Seeing Bobby in a comatose state, Juhi was petrified he was going through a similar feeling. 'In that moment, I felt a very deep connection with him, almost like we were one,' she remembers.

Some doctors had told her that only one in a million people woke up from the condition he was in, and that even if he did come out of coma, there was no assurance that Bobby would be the same lively person he had been. 'I would sit in the ICU, holding his hand and praying, day after day, night after night, just so my brother would be reassured that someone was there beside him and would not be afraid like I used to be; that if he woke up, he would not be alone,' she murmurs.

After a month in this dark place by his bedside, overcome by fear and exhaustion, Juhi broke down. Weeping uncontrollably, she remembered how after losing their parents, Bobby and she had thought that they would always be there for each other. 'That day, I told my inert, almost lifeless brother, that with both our parents gone, we had no other family left. It was just us. "But I can't see you like this anymore, Bobby, it's heart-breaking. If you need to go, go. I will be alright, don't worry about me. Please go, Bobby, but don't be like this…" I urged. Imagine my surprise when, soon after, I saw him stir and try to rise from the bed. For a moment, I felt him trying with all his might to reach out, as though to embrace me. But then, he fell back on the bed and went still again,' she shares.

Bobby was in hospital, comatose, for four years. He passed away on 9 March 2014. 'As I was saying my final goodbye to him, I suddenly realized that after that day by his bedside, Bobby had never stirred, never come out of coma. That was the last time we had communicated with each other. Listening to me, perhaps using the last of his strength, he had tried to rise and hug me. He had failed, and given up. But despite me saying so, I hadn't been able to let him go. Till now,' she concludes, overwhelmed by her emotions.

This final passing changed the course of Juhi's life, forever.

2

SUPARN S. VARMA

Singing in the Dark

When journalist turned writer and director Suparn S. Varma decided to direct *Aatma* (2013), the idea was to make a horror film with a difference. Suparn had written films like Hansal Mehta's *Chhal* (2002), Rohit Shetty's *Zameen* (2003) and Feroz Khan's *Janasheen* (2003) before this, and directed *Ek Khiladi Ek Haseena* (2005) and *Acid Factory* (2009). This was the first time he was experimenting with the horror genre and he hadn't set out to make a '*bhootiya kahani*' (ghost story).

'I am a huge Stephen King fan, but the basic premise of *Aatma* is love more than horror… A father's obsessive and possessive love for his young daughter Nia whom he wants with him even after he has departed the world… A mother's equally overpowering love for her daughter whom she is determined to keep safe from her father's spirit even at the cost of her own life. And when these two opposing loves collide, they turn a fairytale into a nightmare,' Suparn points out.

Bipasha Basu had decided against doing another supernatural thriller after Vikram Bhatt's *Raaz 3: The Third Dimension* (2012), but because *Aatma* was unlike the typical horror films which crop up on screen periodically, she ended up saying 'yes' to Suparn instead of the rehearsed 'no' at the end of the narration. Later, the actress pointed out that there are no similarities whatsoever between the two films as far as story, storytelling or even characterization go. Fear, she argued, unlike love and humour, is not a known emotion. 'So, no two directors would express fear in the same way,' she reasoned.

What neither of them were prepared for was the horror to become so real. When they were shooting the scene where her character, Maya, rushes to the office at night, Bipasha was surprised by the sound of someone singing softly during the take. Since they were working with sync sound, she was even more surprised when the sound recordist did not call 'cut', but let the camera roll till the end of the shot. When she pointed this out to Suparn, the surprised film-maker admitted that even he had not heard anything out of the ordinary. Nor for that matter had anyone else present on the set.

They went for a retake and once again, Bipasha distinctly heard someone singing, quite close to her but not visible. And this time she was not alone. An assistant director corroborated what she was saying. 'So, both the sound recordist and I put on our headphones and that's when we too heard the sound of someone humming in the background,' narrates Suparn.

It was a little past midnight and there was no one in the building except for the film unit. They did a thorough check before alerting the security. 'The guards went up and down the stairs, peeped into empty rooms, and returned to report that they had not come across any trespasser in the Vashi high-rise that housed several offices and was bustling during the day, but eerily silent at night,' he reminisces.

After that there was only one thing left to do. The director emptied out the shooting area with only a few technicians, besides Bipasha and him, staying back on the twentieth floor. The others went down and waited in the lobby or the parking lot, alert to the presence of any strangers. 'But when we resumed shooting, we could still sense an invisible presence around us. Bipasha even joked that somebody else had joined us. Since there wasn't too much we could do, we steeled ourselves and finished the work for the night,' Suparn recounts.

This was not his first brush with the paranormal. Earlier, while shooting for *Acid Factory* in Ramoji Rao Film City, Suparn had sensed someone in the room with him while staying in Sitara Hotel. The sprawling film studio in Hyderabad is said to be haunted by the spirits of soldiers who had died in the many wars fought during the Nizam's reign. They keep the guards on their toes at night. Even during the day, actors have reported seeing another reflection beside their own in the mirror while getting ready for a shot. Lightmen too have complained of someone trying to push them off the parapet while chandeliers have suddenly crashed to the floor and food strewn around by unseen pranksters.

'Nothing happened during the shoot, but on the first night, I returned to my room after pack-up, and I immediately knew that I was not alone. Whoever was there wanted me to switch off the lights without saying it aloud. Once I had doused them, I enjoyed a good night's sleep. This went on for a couple of days after which I had an uneventful stay in that hotel where I stayed for a month without moving to another room,' Suparn narrates.

Another room, in the basement of a Mumbai college, also brings back an eerie memory. This again goes back to the *Aatma* shoot, when they had turned that room into a judge's chamber at the family court where Maya and her husband Abhay's divorce petition is being heard. Abhay, played by Nawazuddin Siddiqui, has bouts of violent rage which results in him losing his job and physically abusing his wife, whom he suspects of having an extramarital affair. Finally, a traumatized Maya files for divorce, asking for sole custody of their daughter. Angry and upset, Abhay threatens to take Nia away in court. The judge, realizing what Maya is going through, pronounces the judgment in her favour and Abhay falls apart. He dies soon after in a car accident but then returns for Nia.

'It was a night shoot and there was a photograph of Dr Babasaheb Ambedkar right behind the judge's chair. We were in the middle of a shot when the picture, which was hanging on the wall, suddenly started to slide to the ground,' remembers Suparn, adding that before it could hit the floor or they could make a grab for it, it stopped its downward plunge and straightened on its own. 'It moved to the left, then to the right, before finding its earlier position. Then, before our startled eyes, it hung itself back in the same place. All this happened within a space of around thirty seconds and we all just stood there silently and gaped; it was so extraordinary. I still haven't found a logical explanation for what we saw that night. All I know for sure is that it wasn't anyone playing pranks because the whole team was right there and everyone was flummoxed. Had someone told me this, I wouldn't have believed it myself, but I have the footage on film,' Suparn shares.

Did the Vashi office or the Kandivali College have a reputation of being haunted? 'No, they were regular places, frequented by office goers and college students during the day. No one had ever reported the presence of an *aatma* (spirit),' he signs off.

3

BISWAJIT

Conversations with a Ghost

'You know after my first Hindi film, I was dubbed the "Suspense Hero from Bengal" by journalists,' veteran actor Biswajit says, laughing. The film in question, *Bees Saal Baad* (1962), was inspired by the Bengali thriller *Jighansa* (1951), which itself was rooted in the Arthur Conan Doyle novel, *The Hound of the Baskervilles*, which was turned into a film in 1939, with Basil Rathbone as Sherlock Holmes. Neither of the Indian adaptations however featured the novel's ferocious hound with the venomous fangs, let loose in the dead of night as part of a diabolical plot.

Bees Saal Baad revolves around Kumar Vijay Singh, played by Biswajit, who comes to Chandanghat as the new *jagirdar* to get to the bottom of a curse which had lured his father and uncle to their death in the surrounding swamp. Soon after moving into the *haveli*, he hears the sound of *ghungroos* at night, beckoning him from the marshy land, and a haunting voice luring him towards his doom.

A cave set had been built in Mumbai's Filmistan Studio by art director Biren Nag, who was making his directorial debut with the Hemant Kumar production. That's where the scenes in the swamp were shot, with real bats flying over Biswajit's head and snakes hanging from the creepers. Every time the actor walked on the set and brushed past a hissing reptile, he was afraid he would not live to see another day.

He survived the ordeal, and the following year, turned up in another suspense thriller, *Bin Badal Barsaat* (1963), which again revolves around a curse and a vengeful spirit. In this film, Biswajit's character, Prabhat, is in love with Asha Parekh's Sandhya, who is ready to marry him even after being told that all the thakur wives had died soon after the wedding. The third angle in this love triangle is Nishi, a reincarnated gypsy girl, who is determined to marry Prabhat, whose father uses black magic to bring him to her when he is asleep.

'The scenes in which I am sleepwalking towards Nishi's home required hours of rehearsal to look convincing on screen. Perhaps, I was a little too diligent because one night, I actually walked out of my bedroom and out of the house. I was about to step into the street when my security guard spotted me near the gate and came running,' Biswajit reminisces.

The guard was surprised to see his sahab leaving home in his pajamas, looking dazed and disoriented. 'His concerned questions broke the spell and I came awake with a jolt. Sending him off to get me a glass of water so I would have some time to compose myself and come up with a believable explanation, I thanked my lucky stars that Ram Singh had seen me else I could well have met with an accident.' The actor shudders at the memory.

What happened during the shoot of *Kuheli* (1971) was even more eerie. In Tarun Majumdar's Bengali film, Biswajit is cast as a widower with a young daughter, who is drawn to the adjacent forest every night by a woman singing. While the locals believe it is a ghost, the young girl is convinced it is her dead mother.

They were shooting in Kalimpong and one evening, after dinner, borrowing his overcoat from the film's wardrobe department, the actor decided to go out for a stroll. Preoccupied, he had walked quite a distance before his aching feet stopped him from going further. Wearily, he turned back towards the hotel, squaring his shoulders for the long trek, when he spotted a car parked by the side of the road. He could see the driver at the wheel and hoping to get a lift, he approached it. 'But when I tapped on the window, no one responded. So then, I peered into the dark interiors and found to my surprise that the car was empty,' Biswajit flashbacks to that spine-chilling moment. Disappointed, he walked away, but he had gone only about ten steps when something made him glance back uneasily over his shoulder. 'The car was still there and it was not empty. I could clearly see the silhouette of a man sitting inside,' he recounts.

This time he didn't think of going back, but kept walking. 'Every time I looked back over my shoulder, I could see the car was still parked there. It was only after I was inside the hotel, that I could breathe again,' the actor admits. To this day, Biswajit is unable to say for certain if there was really a man in that car or if it was just a figment of his imagination. 'Maybe it was a ghost,' he murmurs, almost to himself.

There was another incident on the sets of a film whose name he can't recall. And this time no one was left in any doubt that it was a ghost. 'One day, I noticed that our art director was looking disturbed and beckoning him over, I asked Shiv Shankar what the matter was,' Biswajit narrates.

The man, he learnt, was upset because his young nephew had contracted a mysterious illness and was wasting away every day. He asked for the boy to be brought to the set the next day. 'One look at him, so thin, disoriented and drowsy, and I was convinced that he was possessed,' asserts Biswajit.

Speaking in a loud voice, his tone authoritative, he tried to provoke the spirit into confiding in him. Everyone on the set, including the boy's father, was surprised by his repeated queries to someone no one could see. There was no response and the boy continued to sit there, his head lolling, despite his father's constant reprimands to sit up and answer sahab's questions.

After a while, Biswajit's tone grew softer and more conciliatory. His palms folded in supplication, he entreated the spirit to let the youngster go. Again, he was met with studied silence. Then, when everyone was beginning to get restless and worry for his sanity, the boy started speaking, in the thin, quivering voice of an old lady. His grandmother.

She was livid because the boy's father, her son, had not come to see her when she was dying despite her pleas to liberate her soul with one last drop of water. 'I died parched and haven't found any peace since,' she complained bitterly, insisting that now having taken possession of her grandson's body, she would take him away with her.

She was finally coaxed to let the boy live, after her son promised to perform her last rites, giving her the *Ganga jal* (holy water) that she had been craving for. 'She promised that if he did, she would let the boy go,' says the actor, who gave the man a pen and paper so he could note down her instructions and follow them to the T. 'He did, and within a couple of months, the boy was normal,' he concludes his ghost story.

Biswajit is not scared of *bhoots,* but he has come to fear the power some inexplicable force can exert over one's body, mind and actions. In 1964, he reunited with the *Bees Saal Baad* team of Hemant Kumar, Biren Nag and Waheeda Rehman for *Kohraa* (1964). With his Laurence Olivier-like moustache and his princely good looks, as the aristocratic Raja Amit Kumar Singh, he looked every inch a desi Maxim de Winter from Daphne du Maurier's 1938 novel which had inspired Alfred Hitchcock's Oscar-winning film *Rebecca* (1940).

The Raja falls in love with Waheeda Rehman's Rajeshwari, marries her and brings her to his foreboding mansion which is said to be haunted by the spirit of his first wife, Poonam, who died a year ago, under mysterious circumstances. A few weeks later, after her husband leaves for a business trip, Rajeshwari sets about trying to discover the secret that binds him to the past and his first wife.

They were filming the sequence where the Raja drives his car with Poonam's dead body to the top of the cliff, then jumps out at the last minute, leaning over to watch the car go over the cliff and disappear into the water below. 'Perhaps, I was tired or maybe I was disoriented from watching the car, but I suddenly felt dizzy and collapsed. As everyone crowded around, pulling me away to safety, I realized that had I taken another step, I would have followed the car down the cliff,' Biswajit whispers, still shaken by what could have been a fatal fall.

Another terrifying memory which makes him break out in cold sweat is associated with Darshan Sabharwal's supernatural drama, *Yeh Raat Phir Na Aayegi* (1966). In this film too, his character, Suraj, is torn between Rita, the woman he loves (Mumtaz), and Kiranmayee (Sharmila Tagore). The latter had been a courtesan during the Magadh era, and after her skeleton is excavated, she returns from the dead to lay claims to Suraj, her lover from another life, drawing him towards her with the song '*Yeh woh jagah hai, yehi woh fiza*'. So great is her hypnotic pull that even after he is locked in by Rita's father, Suraj smashes a pane and climbs out of the window to get to his Kiranmayee.

Against the wishes of his director, Brij Sadanah, Biswajit had insisted on doing the scene himself. 'I wasn't actually supposed to smash the glass, but something kept telling me I had to do it. And before I knew it, I had driven my fist through that windowpane. The glass shattered and suddenly, there was blood everywhere,' he remembers.

He had cut a vein and needed stitches to stem the gush of blood. When Brij reprimanded him for his foolishness, his hero muttered that it was an accident. 'But deep down, I knew it had been no accident. There had been something … someone … inside me, telling me I had to break the glass and get out,' Biswajit confides.

4

JOY BIMAL ROY

Don't Buy This Property!

'Would you believe it, my mother had been warned against buying the property where we currently reside, a couple of years before it was available for sale,' informs film-maker Bimal Roy's son Joy.

He goes on to narrate that back then, they had rented Godiwala Bungalow, which was on the same property as the cottage in which they live now. It was owned by the Godiwalas on Bandra's Mount Mary Hill, a sylvan suburb in Mumbai. The bungalow was huge, with a dining room which was like a cottage in itself. Separate from the main house, it could be accessed from the back too. One night, his mother, Manobina Roy, dreamt that she was alone in the dining room, checking the arrangements for the dinner they were hosting that evening, when two elderly Parsi women suddenly walked into the room.

'Maa was not really surprised because strangers had a way of turning up at our home, and she simply looked at them inquiringly. One of them looked her straight in the eye and told her not to buy the cottage which stood on the same property, warning her that it would bring bad luck. And then, maa woke up,' Joy recounts.

Years later, he learnt that Nusserwanji Pestonji Godiwala, who had built the house, had given the cottage to his two unmarried Parsi sisters to live in. This was long before Bimal Roy and his family moved into Godiwala Bungalow. 'Maybe maa saw the sisters, who were long dead by then, in her dream, come to warn her against the property,' Joy surmises.

A couple of years later, the landlady who was a close friend of his mother, requested Manobina to persuade her husband to buy the cottage. 'Bina, you can't be a tenant all your life, tell Bimal to buy the cottage; it will be a good legacy to leave your children,' she cajoled.

The problem was that the film-maker had an aversion to owning property after a painful past experience. 'My grandfather had a huge ancestral property in Bangladesh, but much like Amjad Khan's Nawab Wajid Ali Shah in Satyajit Ray's period drama *Shatranj Ke Khiladi* (1977), my *dadu* too had spent his days playing *daba* (a board game) with his younger brother, unmindful of worldly matters. Taking advantage of this, the estate manager connived to get the property transferred to his own name,' informs Joy.

When his grandfather passed away, while his father's older siblings were already settled and living elsewhere, his grandmother and a young Bimal Roy, along with his two younger brothers, were thrown out by the estate manager with just the clothes on their back. 'Baba was in his teens when they came to Kolkata to make a new beginning. Since then, he believed that property only brings unhappiness which was why even after becoming a well-known film-maker, he continued to rent the bungalow,' Joy explains.

However, his mother was tempted by the offer because the cottage was on prime property. In fact, there were plenty of takers for it. Reportedly, even the playback singer Mohammed Rafi had made an offer for it, but the Godiwalas were a conservative Parsi family and only wanted to sell the cottage to someone they knew. 'That's how Miss Papa, the landlady, a descendant of the Godiwalas, who was very close to my mother, came to approach her. Maa took baba's manager, Amrit Shah, into confidence, and together, they made a plan to buy the property,' Joy narrates.

Since they did not have the money to pay outright, an agreement was drawn up and the land was mortgaged back to the owners. It was mutually agreed that the Roys would settle the sum in small monthly instalments over three years. 'When it came to paperwork, my father trusted Mr Shah implicitly. He blindly signed all cheques and agreements vetted by him without going over them. So, it was only three years later, when the last instalment was due and the sum was a little larger than normal, that looking at the amount baba asked Mr Shah what the money was for while signing the cheque. Mr Shah gleefully informed him that he was now the proud owner of a property in Bandra,' reminisces Joy.

His father was livid, telling his manager that he did not make films to buy property, but to put the money back in films. 'Apologizing for keeping him in the dark all these years, Mr Shah reasoned that all his peers had not just bought properties in Bombay (now Mumbai) but even farmhouses on the outskirts of the city while he had nothing to his name till then. Baba acknowledged that Mr Shah had always had his best interests at heart but still did not speak to him for three days.'

Then, realizing that it was too late to step back, the property deed was signed and the Roys became the owners of the cottage and the property around it in 1962. However, since it was a little too small for the family, they continued to live in the more spacious Godiwala bungalow. The cottage was leased out to Siemens.

On 8 January 1966, at the age of fifty-six, Bimal Roy succumbed to cancer. Soon after, his wife learnt that they had to pay the income tax department Rs 9 lakh in arrears. It wasn't a case of tax evasion, Joy is quick to add. 'My father's film *Sujata* (1959) had been granted tax exemption, but later, the government revised the order and my father was charged not just entertainment tax for the film, but also penalized for not paying the tax,' he explains.

Since they had never seen that kind of money in their lives, the cottage, which was their only asset, was attached by the income tax department. When his mother tried to argue her case, she was told that it would be returned once the arrears were paid, failing which they would sell it to recover their dues. The feisty Manobina reached out to Morarji Desai, Second Deputy Prime Minister and Minister of Finance, and even Indira Gandhi, who was the prime minister then, as also the income tax commissioner, and pleaded her case. Eventually, she succeeded in getting the amount scaled down to Rs 1 lakh, but since her husband had died without leaving a will, she could not access his money till a letter was issued naming her as the administrator. 'When the order finally came in, she discovered that there was exactly Rs 1 lakh in the account, just the right amount to get the property released,' shares Joy.

However, their problems did not end there because soon after, the landlord moved court to have Manobina and her children evicted from Godiwala Bungalow. The Siemens' lease had expired in 1969 and the cottage was vacant, except for a couple of months when Joy's uncle, a well-known artist, and his German student had stayed there. 'They insisted that they had heard someone pacing up and down the veranda at night, but when they opened the door and went out to check, there was no one there. Nevertheless, my uncle was convinced the cottage was haunted and I remember going with him and hammering some nails into a tamarind tree outside it as it was believed that doing this keeps spirits away,' reminisces Joy.

Meanwhile, the case was still going on, and on the advice of their lawyer, the cottage was rented out as it could go against them legally if left vacant. Unfortunately, their first tenant, who was a good man, was suddenly transferred to Kolkata. Manobina, who was already frazzled by all the problems that had fallen on her, asked him to find her a tenant before leaving. 'He suggested someone he didn't know personally, and to our bad luck, his successor turned out to be a rogue. We had to file a case to evict him, finally getting back the property in 1976,' Joy informs, admitting that the property is embroiled in legal problems to this day.

He moved into the cottage in 2002 with his elder sister, costume designer and art director Yashodhara Roy. After her demise in January 2020, another sister, Aparajita, has shifted there from Hyderabad and they reside with a couple of household help and a family of cats and a dog. 'It's a beautiful place, but like the Parsi ladies had warned, it hasn't given us much peace,' he sighs.

You wonder if he has seen or felt any presence living there and Joy admits he hasn't. 'Our family has always been very respectful towards spirits and never tried to force them out of our land. Perhaps that's why they have never harmed me or my people,' he surmises.

He goes on to reveal that intuition runs in the family and he too has sensed ghosts elsewhere. One incident happened when he had gone to Kolkata for a cousin's wedding. They had rented out the palace of the Maharaja of Burdwan for the marriage ceremony, a common practice in Bengal. On the day of the wedding, Joy went there with a few members of the family to check out the place and the arrangements.

'It was a grand mansion, with a huge garden at the back and a pond, and as is typical with many old houses, gave you the impression that time had stood still. I walked around with the others, inspecting the preparations, and since everything seemed to be in order, I wandered off to explore the place on my own. As I was walking down a long corridor, I suddenly recoiled, overcome by a wave of malevolence. It was morning, around 11 a.m., yet the corridor was dark and felt distinctively evil. I turned and hurried back to the others,' Joy recalls.

Later he learnt that the maharaja had murdered one of his servants and dumped him in the garden. 'He could have been killed in that very corridor, which led to the kitchen and offered a view of the pond, which was perhaps why I had felt those negative vibes,' he muses.

One of Joy's sisters and a cousin are also psychic, as was his mother. He remembers when they had gone on a vacation to Shillong in Meghalaya, his mother had stepped into the hotel room they had booked for her and flatly refused to stay there. She insisted that she felt an evil presence in the room. 'Eventually, maa and three of us siblings crowded into one room. It wasn't a comfortable arrangement, but we later learnt that someone had actually died in that hotel room she had refused to occupy,' he informs.

Joy also shares, that like his mother and sister, he also had the gift of auto-writing and could communicate with spirits. 'There's a feeling of restlessness and then, on its own, the right hand grows heavy and starts to write. The words flow easily from another realm on to the paper,' he explains, adding that when Nabendu Ghosh, who had scripted several of his father's films, including *Parineeta* (1953), *Biraj Bahu* (1954), *Devdas* (1955), *Yahudi* (1958), *Sujata* (1959) and *Bandini* (1963), heard this, he advised Manobina, Joy and his sister not to practice it, pointing out that they could inadvertently attract some evil spirit who might harm them. Joy's auto-writing came to a permanent halt thereafter.

Today, Godiwala Bungalow has been razed, and a well that was on the property was sealed, to make way for a sixteen-floor skyscraper. There is a story behind that well too. Joy recalls that a few years after they had moved into the bungalow, from the window, his mother saw the gardener sprinkling what looked suspiciously like blood behind the kitchen. 'Turned out it was blood, and when maa questioned him, the *mali* told her matter-of-factly that a couple had jumped into the well and committed suicide. To appease their ghosts, who were said to reside in the well and believed to be vengeful, the landlords had told him to kill a chicken and sprinkle its blood all over the property. Apparently, it was an annual ritual. Maa was no stranger to ghosts herself, but this was a little too close and morbid for her comfort,' Joy chuckles weakly, admitting that after she narrated the story to them, the children steered clear of the well.

After his father bought the property, he felt that the cottage, which was empty at the time, needed some security to prevent it from being vandalized at night or becoming a meeting place for miscreants. So, the same gardener was asked to sleep on the veranda. A few days after he started doing this, the mali came banging on the front door of Godiwala Bungalow early one morning looking absolutely terrified.

He was almost incoherent at first. When his torrent of words finally began to make sense, they gathered that a couple had appeared to him in a dream. The man, he informed, was dressed in a suit while the *memsahib* was in a dress. 'Both were really angry to find me on their property and told me that since I was a trespasser, they were going to throw me out. When I woke up, I found myself lying in the garden,' the gardener blabbered.

Joy remembers his parents trying to reassure him, telling him it had just been a dream and there was no reason to panic. But the mali absolutely refused to stay there even a minute longer, insisting that his life was in danger. 'We had no way of knowing if what he had told us was the truth or a figment of his imagination. We gave him the benefit of doubt and did not venture near the cottage. The ghosts had the run of the land,' he quips.

Then, around 1967–68, after his father's untimely demise, one of the coconut trees standing by the well weakened at the roots and tilted, leaning precariously against another palm next to it. Afraid that it might fall any day and injure someone, the landlords sent word to men living in the slum behind them to cut it. 'We had a maid working for us who lived in that slum. Her husband was convalescing from jaundice. She had finished her work and left, but then came running back when she learnt that her husband had come with the other men to chop the tree,' Joy narrates.

The maid was worried because her husband was still ailing and had been asked to rest. He wasn't supposed to be outdoors and she had come to drag him home. But before she could collar him, a tragedy happened. 'From what she told us later, he had been leaning over the well, and peering at something in the depths of the well, when the uprooted palm suddenly toppled over and fell on him, killing him on the spot. After his sudden death, some believed that he had been a human sacrifice of sorts to the ghosts, adding drama to the well which by then had earned the reputation of being haunted and was later sealed.'

Years later, when Joy had gone to his friend Miniya's house for dinner, he met a lady there. After dinner, when they were smoking companionably in the balcony which overlooked Godiwala Bungalow, which was right across the road, she looked in its direction and told him that the house had once belonged to her boyfriend's family, the D'Ga-s. She added that his grandfather, weighed down by gambling debts, had committed suicide in the bungalow.

When Joy protested, saying he lived there and that both the bungalow and the cottage had been built by Nusserwanji

Pestonji Godiwala, whose initials NPG were inscribed on the main gate, she insisted that her boyfriend had pointed out the house to her from the gate and told her its history. 'I returned home with the seeds of doubt planted in my mind and decided to check the sale document. That's when I discovered that she had been right. A D'Ga had indeed sold the property to Nusserwanji. And at long last I learnt the identity of our resident ghosts, Mrs and Mr D'Ga,' he concludes.

5

RAJNIESH DUGGALL

Baba to the Rescue

It was just another day's shoot for the team of the romcom, *Direct Ishq* (2016), filming in a haveli in Varanasi. Many others had shot there before them as the location is popular with Hindi film-makers. One night, Rajniesh Duggall, with co-stars Arjun Bijlani and Nidhi Subbaiah, was filming inside one of the rooms while the make-up artist sat outside under a tree, her long hair open, enjoying the cool breeze, waiting to be summoned.

Suddenly, her scream jolted them, bringing work to a stop. Some members of the crew ran out to find her looking absolutely terrified. She admitted that something out there had scared her out of her wits, but since she seemed otherwise okay, no one was unduly perturbed.

Soon after, 'pack-up' was announced and no one gave the incident much thought, till the girl she was sharing the room with informed them the next day that the make-up artist appeared to be ill. 'She looked it too, with pronounced dark circles ringing her eyes which had a dazed and disoriented look, as if she was high on alcohol or drugs,' recalls Rajniesh.

A doctor was summoned to attend to her while the rest of the team went off to shoot. 'Her condition didn't improve despite the medication and on the third day, when someone went to call her, they found her under the bed, telling them in a man's voice to go away,' he continues.

A priest was summoned and a *puja* performed. It didn't help. They even got an exorcist, but even he couldn't cure her. 'That's when the line-producer suggested we take her to Assi Ghat, to the *aghori babas* who practice post-mortem rituals. He suspected she had been possessed,' shares Rajniesh.

The aghoris are a small bunch of ascetic Shaiva *sadhus* who live in charnel grounds. Many are revered among the locals for their healing powers acquired through eremitic rites.

Rajniesh, along with a production hand, their DoP (Director of Photography) Suresh Beesaveni, and the film's director, Rajiv S. Ruia, carried the struggling girl to the Ghat. They were surprised that though she was ailing, she possessed superhuman strength and almost broke free of their hold several times during the journey.

'We somehow managed to get her to a baba. As he smeared cremation ashes on her forehead, strange sounds started coming out of her throat. In response to his queries, she said that she was a raja and despite his repeated requests, refused to leave the girl's body,' the actor narrates.

The baba then told them to carry her down to the river and dip her in the Ganga three times. Knowing how strong she could be, and afraid that the spirit would overpower them this time, they were wary. He then instructed two aghoris to take her. 'After the third dip, something black flew out of her mouth, just like you see it happen in horror movies, and she fainted. We brought her back to the hotel, fearing the worst. But surprisingly, the next day, she was absolutely fine and nothing untoward happened for the rest of the shoot,' Rajniesh concludes.

Enquiries revealed that a king had once lived in the haveli, but no such incident had been reported before this. Or since. While some will scoff at this ghost story and dismiss it as the product of an active imagination, the actor swears by it because not only did it happen right in front of his eyes, but, as he confides, he had learnt at a very young age that spirits do exist.

'Ours is a large joint family, and while it was fun to have so many cousins to play with, being the youngest, I was often bullied by them too. My brothers and sisters would force me to sit in front of the television and watch horror films like *Kabristan* (1988). They even took the cushions away, so I did not have anything to cower behind,' he reminisces with a laugh.

This continued till Rajniesh was in the fourth or fifth standard when his mother taught him the *Hanuman Chalisa*. 'Once I started reciting the devotional hymn, I felt empowered and was never scared again,' he admits.

However, his aunt was terrified by what happened during a vacation in Shimla. Four families had gone together and stayed at a hotel which had some floors below street level as is common in hill stations. Late one night, after dinner, the children were still playing on the minus two level while the adults had retired to their rooms on the floor below when a scream had them racing down.

'My *bua* (aunt) was crying and shivering in the arms of my uncle who was telling her reassuringly, "Sweety, *sab theek ho jayega* (Everything will be alright),"' recounts Rajniesh, who was in the seventh standard then and around twelve years old. In answer to their queries, they learnt that she had been in the bathroom—a long, narrow room—washing her face, brushing her teeth and getting ready for bed when a sound had her turning to the left. As she had watched wide-eyed, a woman had come out of the wall, crossed the room and passed through the wall on the right, disappearing from sight. 'She did not speak to her, touch or harm her, but bua was naturally spooked,' he rewinds.

Years later, when the actor returned to Shimla and made enquiries about the hotel whose name he doesn't recollect now, he was told that it had shut down. Several other hotels there had also downed shutters following such paranormal sightings or hauntings.

Rajniesh, who has a degree in commerce from the Delhi University, and is a graduate in business administration, won the title of Grasim Mr India in 2003. The same year, he represented India at the Mr. International contest in London where he was runners-up. Two years later, he was Kingfisher's 'Model of the Year'. After a couple of remix music videos, including Bombay Vikings' *Chhod Do Aanchal* and *UMI 10 Volume 5* in 2004 and 2005, he debuted in films with Vikram Bhatt's period horror romance *1920* (2008). He plays Arjun Singh Rathod who vows to save his wife, played by Adah Sharma, after they move into a haunted house and she is possessed. Loosely inspired by the iconic Hollywood horror film, *The Exorcist* (1973), it spun a series, *1920: Evil Returns* (2012), *1920: London* (2016), *1921* (2018) and *1920: Horrors of the Heart* (2023).

1920 was shot in Allerton Castle, a nineteenth-century Victorian-Gothic house, which had belonged to the Mauleverer family during the Norman Conquest. It has changed hands many times since and was rebuilt twice, in 1740 and 1789. In 1843, it was demolished again and architect George Martin was engaged to build the present Tudor-Gothic-style castle. Money ran out and work came to a halt thirteen years later. During the Second World War, Allerton Castle was the headquarters of the Royal Canadian Air Force, which operated from there in 1965 too.

In 1983, the house was sold to an American businessman, Dr Gerald Rolph, who renovated and refurbished it. But a fire in 2005 caused substantial damage to the north wing. The castle is now run by the Gerald Arthur Rolph Foundation for Historic Preservation and Education. Rooms and the grounds are available for corporate events, weddings and shoots.

Several television shows and films have been shot there, among them the tele film *Sherlock Holmes: The Sign of Four* (1987), an episode of the television series *Sherlock Holmes* (1984), ITA's British series *Lost in Austen* (2008), Channel 4's comedy-drama *Utopia* (2013) and Season 2 of ITV's *Victoria* (2017).

Vikram Bhatt chose it as the setting for *1920* and Rajniesh admits that some of the rooms, in particular the washroom, gave him cold vibes. If rumours are to be believed, a carpenter was killed there and his spirit haunts the place now.

The caretaker had warned the cast and crew never to go alone to the one washroom they had permission to use. It was in the basement, about twelve to fifteen steps down. 'You had to walk down a long passage to reach it and it was pretty scary.

We would only go down in groups and even then, it gave us the shivers,' the actor says.

One day, while they were sitting around chatting, someone told the executive producer, Manmohan Singh, that there was a ghost in the bathroom. The EP scoffed and said he would go down alone that very minute to prove it was nothing more than a rumour.

'Mohan-ji stomped off and returned ten to fifteen minutes later, his hair dishevelled, his clothes slightly torn, shivering and stuttering,' remembers Rajniesh. Apparently, he had descended the stairs and walked down the alley, the lights coming on automatically. But once he neared the toilet, they flickered and went off completely when he was inside. 'Then, a pair of hands encircled him from the back, trying to tear off his clothes and molest him.'

When the caretaker heard about the incident, he reminded them of his warning and confided that some of the carpenters when working below had also complained of the unwelcome attention of someone they couldn't see but could feel. 'It turned out that these incidents had only ever happened with men,' Rajniesh adds.

The owner of the castle, an old doctor who looked to be in his nineties, also intimidated them. He usually kept to himself, away from the shoot, but having heard that he was fond of Indian food, one of the assistant directors had gone up on the first day and invited him to join them for lunch. He had turned the boy away brusquely, but after a while, came down quietly, piled his plate high with food and returned to his room.

'A little later, he was back, filling up his plate again. This happened around four times. After that he was down every day during meals, all through the duration of our shoot at the castle. Since he was a skinny, elderly gentleman whose wife had passed away, and he didn't have any other family living with him, we naturally wondered about his huge appetite but did not probe for fear of offending him,' says Rajniesh.

One has read of his co-stars, Adah Sharma and Anjori Alagh, being spooked out by certain rooms in the castle. He acknowledges all the stories are true. 'It's something I never felt while filming *Dangerous Ishhq* (2012) in Jodhpur's Mehrangarh Fort or *Ek Paheli Leela* (2015) at the Laxmi Niwas Palace in Bikaner or even while at the Khimsar Fort which is perched on the edge of the Thar desert. Both those films were reincarnation dramas, but there were no undercurrents of fear on the sets. *Phirr* (2011) and *Saansein* (2016) also did not give me any anxious moments despite being horror films,' Rajniesh asserts, but admits that he was terrified while at Allerton Castle.

Once he posed with his wife Pallavee and some members of his staff in front of the portrait of the owner and his wife. 'When the photographs were developed, while our faces were clear, the frame behind us was blank,' he shivers.

The actor confides that he believes he is a receiver or a medium. He has read up on the subject and spends a lot of time in mediation, asserting that while this life is our chance to do good and improve our karma, it's not the end of our existence. 'There are different realms so yes, there are spirits around us whom we can't see,' he says.

Rajniesh himself is very sensitive to vibes, and if they are not good, he doesn't hang around the place. He is quick to add that not all spirits are bad. 'My nani (grandmother) died when I was in the eleventh standard and over the last twenty-two years, I have felt her protective aura surrounding me without ever being afraid. A couple of others have also noted her presence, and once, someone actually mentioned that there was someone else in the room with me. In response to my "Who?", he informed me that she was a grey-haired woman with bluish-grey eyes,' he shares, revealing that his nani had distinctive bluish-grey eyes, but since he has never spoken about her in any of his interviews, no one would have known this.

Rajniesh can also communicate with his late father and his mother-in-law, who was suffering from cancer and passed away at the age of fifty-one. 'My wife Pallavee and I were very close to her, and after her untimely demise, we went to Shiamak Davar (dancer-choreographer) who knows auto-writing so we could connect with her,' he informs.

Shiamak told the actor that even he has the gift of connecting with those who are gone, and by helping those they have left behind, he could help his own soul. 'I have since done auto-writing for a few close people, but it drains me of my energy and over time, I have learnt that it's better that we do not inhabit parallel worlds,' Rajniesh asserts.

6

VIKRAM BHATT

Ghost on Camera

On 5 January 2018, at 12.36 p.m., Vikram Bhatt tweeted, 'We caught a ghost on camera! This is no publicity stunt! Scouting for *1921* at Wentworth Woodhouse, which is among the most haunted in the UK, we caught this apparition. The house was owned by a coalminer who is said to haunt the house. We never saw him. The camera did!'

The post was accompanied by a picture of the mansion, which appears dark, gloomy and straight out of a horror movie. If you look closely, you can see a shadowy figure, just below the stairs, near a ground-floor window. The film's writer, producer and director had circled the man whose feet appear to be floating a few inches above the ground, and since he's still just a blur in a long shot, Vikram had zoomed in for a close-up. Interestingly, the team of the reality show, *Most Haunted*, which had shot there too, had reported having seen their first ghost at Wentworth Woodhouse.

The ghost did not scare away Vikram. Not even when on his way to the men's room he had an adventure of his own. 'I had to traverse the area which you may call the most haunted part of the property. My attendant started to walk behind me and I stopped him, saying, "Listen, you don't have to bother, I can go to the loo alone." But as I was walking down, I heard him right behind me and I told myself that this guy was never going to leave,' he reminisces.

The floors were marble and granite and their footsteps had a nice ring to them. When he was near the washroom, Vikram turned around to assure the man that he could manage now. 'And there was nobody there, he had not come with me. That really blew my mind and my thoughts went back to the image we had captured on camera that same morning. It was like a kind of confirmation of what I had gone there looking for,' points out the film-maker, who went back there to film the love story of an impoverished music student, who is possessed by a vengeful spirit, and a ghost whisperer, who is determined to save him, so his music lives on.

1921 (2018) wasn't shot only in the haunted Wentworth Woodhouse. Vikram and his unit also travelled to Downham, a 300-year-old village in Lancashire, which was once home to one of the Pendle witches who was hanged after England's notorious witch trial. They also set a few scenes in Ripley's Castle, one of the most haunted places in Yorkshire's Harrogate. During its 700-year-old history, soldiers of the Civil War were shot dead in the castle by Lord Cromwell's firing squad after the battle of Marston Moor. A Catholic priest, Francis Ingilby, was hung, drawn and quartered there, and then there was the poltergeist, Lady Alice, who had lost two babies to meningitis in 1870 and is said to still get upset when she hears a baby cry, rushing down the long and dark corridors and through locked doors. Vikram had earlier filmed *1920* (2008) at Ripley's Castle for two days in 2007.

The film-maker believes in ghosts and has deliberately travelled across the world, to locations known to be haunted, for his reel-life stories. He was in Transylvania, made famous by Bram Stoker's *Dracula*, for *Raaz: Reboot* (2016). Vikram and his team weren't allowed inside the castle and could only take a few shots from outside, but he did film in the mansion where Romanian dictator Nicolae Ceausescu was apprehended while trying to escape in a helicopter. Subsequently, he was tried by the army and shot dead. The house, now a hotel, which is a fifteen-minute drive through the forest, is believed to be haunted. But fortunately for Vikram, the only hauntings that happened there were scripted by him.

However, there is a real ghost story behind his film, *Ghost* (2019). While researching, Vikram had stumbled upon a show titled *The Haunting*, and learnt about an American by the name of Arne Johnson, who, in 1981, was tried for the murder of his landlord. His lawyer had argued that the man was killed by the devil who had possessed Arne. His novel defence caught the imagination of the local media who had dubbed it 'The Devil Made Me Do It' case. But the judge was not impressed and the case was not admitted by the British court. It set Vikram thinking: If what Arne said was true, how could an innocent man prove that a cold-blooded murder had been committed by a ghost? And that became the premise of *Ghost* (2019).

The film chronicles the high-profile murder trial of a young politician, Karan, accused of killing his wife after CCTV footage shows him entering his apartment at 2 a.m., exiting at 4 a.m., the time when Barkha was killed, and returning at 6 a.m. With all the evidence pointing towards him, Karan is in the dock, literally. It gets worse when the friend in whose apartment he claims to have spent the night, is later killed by the same ghost who murdered Barkha and turns out to be her lesbian partner. It takes a trusting attorney and an exorcism to get him off the hook. The film ends leaving the audience wondering if the curse is really over. Did he catch a ghost on camera during *Ghost* too? 'Yes, I did. I am certain it was an entity,' Vikram admits.

While one doesn't know if *Ghost* will spin a sequel, *1920* (2008) was turned into a franchise with *1920: Evil Returns* (2012) arriving four years later, followed by *1920 London* (2016) and *1920: Horrors of the Heart* (2023).

There's also the *Raaz* series which Vikram flagged off in 2002. He returned to it after a decade with *Raaz: The Third Dimension* (2012), followed by *Raaz Reboot* (2016). Interestingly, a scream from *Raaz* is rooted in a real-life ghost story. Back in the 1990s, he was shooting *Gunehgar* (1995) in Mumbai's Mukesh Mill. It was around 3 a.m. and they were filming an action scene below one of the dilapidated buildings on a street set. At one point, the director decided that he wanted a top-angle shot and entered the building with two camera assistants, two camera attendants and his assistant director.

They walked up to the second floor and into a long room that stretched for about 200–250 feet. Most of it was cloaked in darkness at that hour. 'We set up the camera near the window from where we had a clear view of the action below. I took a chair and sat down. Ten minutes later, we were jolted by a terrible scream of pain, followed by a whispered, "*shh shhh shhh*,"' he recounts.

As they all looked at each other, Vikram's first reaction was that someone was playing a prank on them. But on second thought, he realized that the pain in the voice had been too real. As a chill ran down his spine, he called his action director, Abbas Ali Moghul, and informed him about it. 'Abbas *bhai* had not heard anything, but he sent two burly fighters up to where we were standing huddled together. They took a few steps into the darkness, turned back hurriedly, told us that there was no one there and ran back downstairs,' he continues.

After the shot was taken, they went down and were talking about what had just transpired when a production guy came along with the caretaker. 'The caretaker confided that every night he heard disembodied screams and other strange sounds in the mills,' Vikram informs.

Twelve years later, the film-maker was back at Mukesh Mills for a night shoot of the romantic thriller *Red: The Dark Side* (2007). 'Suddenly, I noticed my executive producer and assistant director almost run out of the same building. When they drew closer, I asked, "You heard a scream, right?" They nodded, looking surprised, and wondered how I knew. I confessed I had heard it too,' he reminisces.

Three years later, when Vikram was working on the post-production of *Raaz*, that scream was still ringing in his ears. Since no one else from that team had heard it, he had trouble making the sound engineers understand what he wanted. He kept rejecting various screams, saying, '*Nahin, yeh woh cheekh nahin thi* (No, this is not that scream).' He finally recreated it himself by mixing together two screams.

With the third instalment of the *Raaz* franchise, he ventured into the dark world of black magic with Bipasha Basu's character,

Shanaya, an actress whose stardom is waning, who makes a pact with the devil to destroy the career of a younger rival and bring her lover back to her. Vikram has never come across black magic rituals or even seen anyone stick pins in voodoo dolls. But he admits that he met a *tantrik* who left him bemused. 'It happened before *1920,* which was a turning point for me professionally. I was facing a lot of problems and someone suggested that I visit a particular baba. He told me that someone was working against me. What was surprising was that he vividly described this person who was well known to me,' the film-maker shares. While the revelation surprised him, the fact that someone would want to harm him, didn't. 'I do believe in positive and negative energies. I don't think they can harm you directly, but when you have too much negative energy around you, you might make decisions which are not good for you and may hurt you,' he points out.

Like the scream, has anything else stayed in his mind? 'I carry images of all my paranormal encounters. Over the years, they have burned themselves into my reality,' Vikram admits. And does writing about ghosts and making films like these give him sleepless nights? 'I have sleepless nights with or without ghosts,' says the film-maker, who sleeps with an idol of Krishna by his bedside. 'I believe in God. And where there is light, there is also darkness, right?'

7

BHUSHAN PATEL

And the Angels Beckoned…

Bhushan Patel did not set out to become a director of horror films. He became one by default. He was Mahesh Bhatt's Director of Photography on films like *Dastak* (1996), *Tamanna* (1997), *Yeh Hai Mumbai Meri Jaan* (1999) and *Kartoos* (1999). After Bhatt's premature retirement from direction, Bhushan moved to television and went on to direct long-running series like *Lipstick* (2002–04), *Aathvan Vachan* (2008–09), *Chandragupta Maurya* (2011–12) and *Dwarkaresh Bhagwan Shree Krishn* (2011–12). Then, his friend of forty years, Vikram Bhatt, with whom he had worked in *Gunehgar* (1995) and *Bambai Ka Babu* (1996), approached him to direct the sequel to his hit period romance, *1920* (2008).

'When we were kids, Vikram and I used to watch horror films like *The Exorcist* (1973) two to three times a week. And every time, we were both terrified despite knowing what was to come,' he reminisces, admitting that even though he was fascinated with the genre, he balked at the idea of helming *1920: Evil Returns* (2012), pointing out to his buddy that he was a cinematographer and not a director. Unfazed, Vikram told him that was actually an advantage because in the horror genre, the camera tells the story. Finally, Bhushan gave in.

The film was a hit. Then, he was cajoled into directing *Ragini MMS* 2 (2014) for Ekta Kapoor. *Alone* (2015) and *Amavas* (2019) followed.

'As a child, I had frequent nightmares and would wake up crying. My grandmother and mother were both very religious and believed that iron kept spirits away. So, my mother put a cast iron Sai Baba idol under my pillow. After that the nightmares faded,' Bhushan confides.

Baba reinforced his faith in God, but he also understood that where there is good, there is evil too. So, the fear remains, and his tryst with cinematic horror has only enhanced that fear. 'But it has helped me as a film-maker because when you feel real terror, you can effectively bring it to the screen and evoke the emotion in your viewers too,' he explains.

Karan Singh Grover, who played the lead opposite Bipasha Basu in *Alone*, has admitted to being so spooked by some of the scary scenes that he began to feel that there was a presence around the set. Revolving around conjoined twins, identical in appearance but with different personalities, who promise to be together till they die, *Alone* was based on a 2007 Thai film by the same name. This in turn was inspired by *My Brother's Keeper*, an episode from HBO's American horror anthology television series *Tales from the Crypt* (1989–96). Bhushan spent a lot of time on the script, Indianizing it, making alterations in the plot and the climax. 'I was successful in amping up the fear factor on screen, but didn't experience anything out-of-the-ordinary off it,' the film-maker admits.

With *Amavas*, a tale of death and possession, he went a step forward, filming it in Goring Castle in West Sussex, London, which is believed to be occupied by spirits. There's been talk of disembodied footsteps and heavy furniture being rearranged when nothing seems out of place inside. Bhushan's leading lady, Nargis Fakhri, admitted to being creeped out when shooting in the haunted castle which had been built by first baronet, Sir Bysshe Shelley, for his grandson, the poet Percy Bysshe Shelley. But before he could move in, the younger Shelley drowned at the age of twenty-nine. His widow, Mary Shelley, author of *Frankenstein*, then sold the castle to her tenant, Vice-Admiral Sir George Brooke-Pechell, RN.

The current owner, Lady Colin Campbell, has been renting it out for shoots. Goring Castle featured in an episode of the American paranormal and reality film series, *Ghost Hunters* (2004–16). Lady Campbell also organizes ghost hunts on the castle grounds during which one can experience glass divination and table tipping, be a part of a group human pendulum experiment and play the Ouija Board.

Bhushan informs that apart from lights flickering and sometimes going off, he did not hear anyone crying, laughing or singing in the castle as has been reported. 'Yes, some unit members did complain about things going missing, then turning up somewhere else, but that could well have been a memory lapse. For me, Goring Castle was just a huge, somewhat neglected home of an old lady and her son,' the director maintains.

Underplaying the usual talk of ghosts wandering around in the dark, Bhushan explains that darkness heightens fear and one starts feeling spooked. 'But ghosts don't have to wait for the sun to go down to venture out,' he points out, adding that he believes that like animals, if you don't hurt, anger or defile them, ghosts won't trouble you. 'But yes, spirits can be territorial,' he admits, reminding you of the witch in *Ragini MMS* who says, 'This is my house, I won't leave it. And if anyone comes in, I won't let them leave either.'

Bhushan lost his father in 2004 and during a puja at home shortly after, a light bulb suddenly started glowing brightly before going off. 'That lamp was in my father's favourite corner, where he would always sit on a rope swing. I cremated the swing along with him because he was so attached to it. I would like to believe that the light glowing suddenly was a sign that he was there with us during the puja,' he muses. Was he scared? 'Why would I be scared? He was my father, even after twenty years I still miss him. If he is around, I know he can only be looking out for me,' the film-maker reasons.

Truth, they say, is stranger than fiction, and in Bhushan's case that's definitely true. At the age of four, he fell gravely ill, with a bout of gastroenteritis, after his birthday party on 12 April 1970. His father, who was working as a cameraman with a German company, was boarding a flight to London from Hamburg when he was informed that his son had been admitted to the All-India Institute of Medical Science (AIIMS).

'I was living in Delhi then with my mother and my sister who is fourteen months younger than me. In hospital, my fever escalated and my temperature went up to 108 degrees Fahrenheit, which can prove fatal, leading to convulsions and death. I needed blood urgently, but I'm a rare group, O Rh negative. Back then, we did not have social media broadcasts, just Doordarshan and the radio, so it was difficult to approach people for blood. My mother was my only donor,' Bhushan shares.

As his temperature rose, he was stripped and placed on a slab of ice. His mother was informed that the boy was sinking. 'What happened next was an out-of-the-body experience from a top-angle crane shot, as you would say in film jargon. I watched my mother slowly walk into the room and proceed towards where I was lying. From that angle, I could not see my face, but I could see that my body was still, too still. As I watched, I suddenly saw some angel-like figures emerge from the opposite corner of the ceiling and float towards me. I knew instinctively that they had come to fetch me. But then, just as I had prepared myself for the inevitable, they looked at each other, turned and disappeared,' he recounts.

Bhushan's condition improved after that. The fever subsided and he survived. Later, his parents learnt that two *mohallas* from where they lived in Lajpat Nagar, a man by the name of Bhushan had passed away that night. 'The incident today reminds me of *Jhuk Gaya Aasman* (1968),' he says.

In the romcom, an angel of death mistakes Rajendra Kumar for his lookalike, a criminal, and he is killed in a car crash. But on reaching heaven they learn that his time is not up yet. To rectify the mistake, the angel returns him to earth, but since his body has already been cremated, resurrects his lookalike who has been shot dead by his own brother a few minutes ago, so his soul can inhabit that body. This sets off a strange chain of events.

'I've heard that Mr Bachchan (Amitabh) also returned from the dead,' Bhushan points out, and one is reminded of an interview the actor had given in *India Today* on 15

October 1982, a day after his discharge from the hospital and two months after a near-fatal knockout punch on the sets of *Coolie* (1983) in Bangalore. Bachchan had confided that on 2 August, the day of the second operation, he had been declared technically dead. His doctor had told him later that he should now ring in his birthday twice, once on 11 October, the day he was born, and once on 2 August, the day he was reborn.

Today, when Bhushan flashbacks to that fateful day, he can't remember much about his stay in AIIMS. He has no memory of the room he occupied or the treatment he received there. 'But three images—my mother entering the room and walking towards my body lying on a slab of ice, the figures floating towards me, playing in the hospital corridor and bouncing the crazy ball my father had got me from Germany—will remain entrenched in my mind forever,' he asserts.

8

JEET GANNGULI

The Gift of Music

It was perfect! A one-bedroom, hall and kitchen apartment in a sylvan suburb in Mumbai. Jeet Ganguli and his wife Chandrani couldn't wait to move in. Once they shifted, the singer and composer got busy with music sittings for an upcoming romcom. Chandrani, who had suffered a bad fall a year ago, had taken leave of absence from her job with the NGO Prayaas, as the pain had escalated. The first week, she was happy doing up their home and Jeet was delighted at how tastefully she had decorated it. But after eight to ten days, he noticed that his wife had grown very quiet and seemed disturbed about something. 'Initially, I thought it was because of the pain and was deeply concerned,' he reminisces.

Around that time, Jeet had bought a Korg piano for his father. Kali Ganguli had been an accordion player, but couldn't play the instrument anymore. 'I thought it would make baba happy, but he only wanted to play the accordion or the harmonium. So, I asked Chandrani, who has a talent for music, to learn how to play it,' he says. Soon after, his wife started taking lessons from Joe Fernandes, who, along with his brother Xavier, was one of the city's famous pianists. Their apartment soon filled with the sound of music.

The piano made Chandrani happy, but Jeet noticed that she still seemed disturbed. When he prodded, she admitted that she couldn't pinpoint exactly what the matter was. She just sensed a presence in the apartment. While he had been afraid of ghosts as a child, his wife is the bravest person he knows which is why her apprehension worried Jeet.

He asked the landlord who lived in the adjacent flat if their apartment had some dark history. He was fobbed off, but Jeet could see that the man was uncomfortable about the subject and that strengthened his conviction that whatever the problem was, it had to do with their new home.

All through the music sitting the next day, his wife was on Jeet's mind. He returned home late at night. After dinner, the couple retired to the bedroom. 'Chandrani was playing the piano in the dark, the music soothed me and I was nodding off when suddenly, she fell heavily against my shoulder, insisting there was someone in the room. I switched on the lights and searched the entire apartment. There was no one there except us. We stayed up the whole night, and the next morning, I approached one of our neighbours, telling him what had transpired the night before and asking about the earlier tenants,' Jeet recounts.

After a lot of coaxing and cajoling, the neighbour confided that the flat had belonged to an elderly lady who had lived there with her son, who was a musician. He had played the violin and the piano but had fallen into bad company, got hooked on drugs and committed suicide in the bedroom. 'After his death, the landlord had got his mother to write the flat in his name and then, had packed her off to an old-age home,' he shares.

Once he learnt this, the singer-composer decided they would not spend another night there. They moved to Chandrani's sister's place and went on a frenetic house hunt. Within three to four days, they had located another apartment and moved out. 'Immediately, things were back to normal,' says a relieved Jeet.

But he couldn't stop thinking of the boy, a fellow musician like him, who had left the world with many of his dreams unfulfilled. 'Perhaps listening to Chandrani play the piano had made him yearn for music again and he had come by,' he muses.

A decade passed by and Jeet had almost forgotten the incident when he landed the fourth instalment of the *Raaz* franchise. When writer and director Vikram Bhatt was narrating the story of *Raaz Reboot* (2016) to him, a tune started playing in his head, a tune he picked out on the piano from which '*Raaz aankhein teri*' was born. Sung by Arijit Singh, it melted many hearts across the world. Jeet believes the song is a gift from the dead musician they had crossed paths with briefly in that apartment fourteen years ago. Another song which remains unforgettable is '*Zindagi chal tera shukriya*'.

One day, producer Mukesh Bhatt called to inform him he was making a film. 'It's a father-daughter story featuring Sanjay (Dutt) and Alia (Bhatt). We are calling it *Sadak 2* and I want you to do the main song,' Jeet was told.

In normal circumstances, he would have been delighted to be doing another film with his godfather, but back then, he was going through a really difficult phase. 'In 2016, my father, who had been my friend and guru, was diagnosed with dementia. In 2017, his illness escalated, and by 2018, he had become aggressive and prone to violent bursts of temper. It was painful to see baba this way and I had taken a break from work because I just couldn't focus on my music,' he explains.

In fact, Jeet had been planning to go to Kolkata and stay with his parents for a while when Mukesh Bhatt called. Chandrani urged him to meet his mentor and somewhat reluctantly, he went to the office where he ran into Mahesh Bhatt who took one look at him and asked quietly, '*Jeet, tu theek hai na*?' (Jeet, are you okay?) And the singer-composer found himself telling the Bhatts all about his father. At the end of his teary-eyed narration, Mahesh told him that he would be giving him tickets to fly to his home town immediately. 'Take your wife and go to Kolkata. Once there, compose a song in front of your father. That will be our song,' he urged. In response to Jeet's mumbled, 'But what is the song situation?', he waved his hands dismissively, saying that wasn't important. 'We need a song for our film, my comeback directorial, and I know only you can make it for us,' the film-maker stated.

The next morning, Jeet and Chandrani flew to Kolkata. A few hours later, he was sitting in front of his father, strumming the guitar as he valiantly tried to compose a tune after months. 'Suddenly, baba looked up, clear-eyed, and told me impatiently that what I was playing was not really a good tune and that I could do better. Hope flared, and for a moment, I thought he was getting better. But shortly after that, he was shouting again and flinging things around.'

That night, around 1.30 a.m., Jeet was playing another tune he had composed to Chandrani when someone started beating on their bedroom door. His wife flung it open, expecting to see her mother-in-law. 'But it was baba telling me proudly, "*Ei to shur*, this is the correct tune." I looked at him disbelievingly and asked somewhat tentatively, "Baba, you like it? *Tumi bhalo hoi gechho*?" (You're okay now?) He gave me a half-smile and murmured in a voice that was dear and familiar, "I'm fine, I just don't like you playing bad tunes in front of me. You have to always give your best, Jeet." Apprehensively, I asked him if he liked this one and he nodded. "It's good, but you need to make it better." Saying this, baba turned and went back to his room, leaving me crying.'

The next morning, he sang the song on the phone to Mahesh Bhatt who immediately instructed him to take the evening flight back to Mumbai. 'We have to record it immediately before we leave for shooting,' he explained. Jeet complied, only to learn the following day that his father's health had taken a turn for the worse and he had been admitted to the PG Hospital ICU in Kolkata where they feared he had suffered a multi-organ failure. 'But as I was singing on the mike, I could sense baba standing beside me and I broke down. The recordist, Pankaj Vora, was surprised to see me crying because except for Bhatt sahab, Mukesh-*ji* and Pooja (Bhatt), I had not confided in anyone that my father was critical,' he shares. 'While we were recording the track, I flew to Kolkata and back as many as eight times, going frequently to check on baba.'

What made it an even bigger a challenge was that this song was sung by three singers. So, one day, he was dubbing with KK, the next, with Jubin Nautiyal, and on the third, with Arijit Singh. 'They all cried when they listened to the scratch I had recorded, telling me they would never be able to sing with so much feeling. I admitted that my heart had been breaking for my father at the time.'

After the song was mixed and edited, Jeet flew to Kolkata and drove straight down to the hospital to see his father who had since suffered a heart attack. 'Baba reached for my hand and his fingers started moving on my palm, as if he was playing the accordion again. Don't ask me why, but I just knew that he was playing "*Zindagi chal tera shukriya.*" An hour later, he was gone, leaving me with the song I have always believed was his last gift to me.'

Back in Mumbai, the lyrics were changed and he was told he would have to re-dub the song. He was much too upset to think about work then, having just lost his best friend. 'I couldn't speak to anyone, couldn't even be near a water purifier because its sound reminded me of the ICU. I was crying all the time. Everyone around me was sympathetic and they told me that I had to hold on to my music, baba would have wanted that,' Jeet recalls.

Chandrani prodded him to call Mukesh Bhatt, who after paying his condolences told him gently, '*Beta, tu aa jaa vapas.*' (Son, come back.) And so, after the funeral and the last rites, Jeet flew back to Mumbai and got back to the business of re-dubbing the song with KK and Jubin. But even after they were done with their recordings, it wasn't over. 'Shreya (Ghoshal), having heard the story of the song from me, wanted to sing it too, as a tribute to my father. Every time I was at the studio recording it, I felt baba's blessings. The situation in the film, the lyrics, all are so closely associated with both our lives,' he points out, humming softly, '*Zindagi chal tera shukriya, shayad mile na tu, kal ke subah.*'

Prod him on whether he believes in premonitions and spiritual visitations and Jeet informs that his mother's grandfather was a *shadok* (priest) in a village temple. Every night after the puja was done, he would cut across the fields on his way home. One moonlit night, he was surprised to see some young boys playing between the stalks. 'Drawing closer, he realized that they did not have a stitch on them,' Jeet recounts. As he walked past them, he heard them chatting amongst themselves. One of them was saying that he would visit a home in the village soon, stay there for three months, and leave. The name of the owner was mentioned and he turned out to be the priest's friend.

'The next moring, my great-grandfather went across to meet his friend. After some small talk, he asked him straight if his daughter-in-law was pregnant. The man looked astounded, wondering how he knew since they hadn't told anyone outside the immediate family,' Jeet recounts.

His fears confirmed, the priest left without telling anyone how he had come upon this knowledge, unsure if anyone would believe his fantastic tale. 'A few months later, his friend was blessed with a grandson. Excited, he organized a huge *mukhe bhaat* (child's first rice-eating ritual) ceremony to which the whole village was invited. My great-grandfather tried telling him it was too early to celebrate, but his friend laughed away his concern. Three months later, the baby died,' Jeet concludes, leaving you chilled to the bone.

9

NEIL NITIN MUKESH

Who's That Girl?

With time, memories fade. But for Neil Nitin Mukesh this one is as real as it happened yesterday. And just as terrifying!

It happened one night, when the actor was driving home from Film City Studio in Mumbai. This was when Neil was working as an assistant director on a Yash Chopra production, *Mujhse Dosti Karoge!* (2002), to learn the ropes of the trade. Those were long days when he would arrive on the sets early and pack up only around 1.30 a.m. Even after the stars and the other technicians had left for home, the assistants would be putting the exposed reels of film into the metal cans, which were stamped and ferried to Yash Chopra's bungalow. 'Only after that could we call it a day,' he shares, quick to add that despite the long, back-breaking hours it was fun being around young actors like Hrithik Roshan, Rani Mukerji and Kareena Kapoor, along with the producer's younger son, Uday Chopra, and choreographer Ahmed Khan, and learning on the job.

On that particular day, they were shooting a wedding sequence and the set was filled with bright colours. Red, green, yellow, blue... Every hue except white, which is considered inauspicious during Hindu weddings, and there were strict instructions from director Kunal Kohli to ensure there was no white anywhere.

The shoot went off well and after packing up, Neil left the deserted studio in the small blue Zen which his father, singer Nitin Mukesh, had bought him to make the commute easier. In the car with him was another assistant, Trishul, who lived near Worli Sea Face. Every night, Neil would drop him on his way home to Malabar Hill and pick him up the next morning.

It was around 2.15 a.m. The night was hazy from a light winter mist and the smoke from the fire the men in the nearby *tabela* (stable) had built to ward off the mosquitoes and keep themselves warm. 'Because of the smog, I was driving slowly, peering through the curtain of darkness. A bus carrying the junior artists and the chorus dancers had left before us. My car was inching along the narrow road with the cans of film in the back,' Neil narrates.

After a while, he picked up speed, eager to get home quickly for a couple of hours of shut-eye before it was back to the grind again. 'Suddenly, about twenty to twenty-five feet away, I saw a woman walking down the road. I couldn't see her face because of the smog, but since she was dressed in a white *salwar-kameez,* she was clearly visible. I thought she was one of the dancers who had missed the bus and was walking home. I was livid with Trishul whose job it was to ensure that everyone left the studio safely. I turned on him angrily, wondering how he could have overlooked her,' he recounts.

To his surprise, his fellow AD insisted he couldn't see anyone. Since Trishul wore high-powered glasses and was blind as a bat without them, Neil assumed that the lady in white was not visible to him in the dark. Back then, even he wore spectacles, but he could see her silhouette, sharp and clear, as she walked just ahead of the car. 'I think we should give her a lift to the main road or even to her home if she lives close by,' he muttered, concerned even as Trishul continued repeating as he peered out of the window, 'What woman are you talking about? I don't see anyone.'

By then Neil had pushed his feet down on the accelerator and the car was going at a speed of forty to fifty kilometres. But to his surprise, the lady continued to maintain a distance of twenty to twenty-five feet between her and the car. 'This was strange because no one can walk faster than a car and we should have passed her by then,' the actor reasons.

When he pointed this out to Trishul, his friend told him firmly not to look in her direction. After he had reiterated this a few times, Neil finally understood what he was trying to say. She was a specter, not a normal human being. 'My complexion is anyway pale, but at that moment. I was as white as Casper, the friendly ghost,' Neil admits with a weak laugh, remembering how desperate he was to get away.

Then, all of a sudden, the lady disappeared. One minute she was walking on the road ahead of them, and in the next, she was gone. 'But before I could heave a sigh of relief, I saw her again, sitting on the back seat of our car. It was just a three-second flash, but her presence was clearly visible in the car mirror.' He shudders at the memory.

Slamming the brakes, Neil turned to Trishul and exclaimed, 'She's here, with us!' To his credit, his friend did not panic, but told him in a tone that demanded to be heard not to look back.

'Then, saying he would drive, Trishul made me switch places with him,' he narrates, admitting even now he gets gooseflesh when he remembers that night, which fortunately for them, ended uneventfully once Trishul took the wheel.

The next day when Neil related what had happened, many others admitted that the same thing had happened with them too. 'It was mostly the technicians and the girls, but they described exactly how it had happened with us.' There was an elderly gentleman on the set. He pointed to the jungles near Aarey, which are said to be full of wild animals and spirits, and advised us that it was best to steer clear of these spots, particularly late at night,' he recalls.

Years later, Neil was in Fiji to shoot a Hindi sci-fi horror thriller, *3G: A Killer Connection* (2013), with co-star Sonal Chauhan and the rest of the unit, including Shantanu Ray Chhibber, who co-wrote the story and screenplay and co-directed the film with Sheershak Anand. Shantanu also plays the role of a priest, Father Patterson, in this bizarre plot which starts with Neil's character, Sam, losing his phone in his excitement to meet his girlfriend, Sheena. He buys a new phone with a 3G connection and almost immediately, things start going wrong for him. He is flooded with mysterious calls from an unknown number, followed by a video of a woman being killed, which threatens his sanity.

One day, they were shooting a dark sequence in a hotel room. The actor had been mentally prepping for the scene for hours. The atmosphere was eerie perhaps because the lights were doused and the big garden, which was visible beyond the windows, was full of shadows. It got worse once they started shooting. When Sonal, who plays Sheena, was facing the camera, Neil began to feel there was someone else besides her in the frame though he could see no one on the monitor.

When it was his shot, Shantanu kept calling 'cut', and at one point even shouted out to an assistant to ask the person to move out of the frame. The constant interruptions unnerved Neil and after five retakes, he asked Shantanu why they were doing the shot so many times. His director informed him that every time they went for take, someone kept popping into the frame behind him. 'Hearing this, I asked to see the footage and sure enough, I could see the silhouette of a woman right behind me. In one shot, the DoP had let the camera roll even after Shantanu had shouted 'cut' and we saw her entering the frame and taking up position behind me as if someone had instructed her to do so.'

Immediately, a search for the mystery woman was launched across the hotel. The security guards didn't find anyone. 'But I saw the footage on camera and so did Shantanu and the others. We know for sure that there was definitely someone there in the room with us that night and it really freaked us out,' says Neil, who even as a child, was fascinated by ghost stories. 'But I never imagined then that I would feature in not one, but two of them myself, and they would be for real,' he concludes with a wry smile.

10

SOHAM SHAH

Get Out of the House!

It all started sometime in 2005–06 when his elderly aunt moved out of the heritage building in South Mumbai where she had spent most of her life and shifted into an apartment in Kandivali.

'One morning, I heard my father, who is a doctor and the head of our extended family, telling my mother how bua was not comfortable in her new home and wanted to move back to their old place. When I prodded, I learnt that someone in a white kurta-pyjama was coming to her in her dreams, every night, at around 2 a.m., telling her to get out of the apartment,' recounts writer-director Soham Shah, admitting that he had laughed out loud when he had heard this seemingly absurd story and joked that she must be seeing his *phufa* (uncle).

That night, Soham himself had a dream in which he saw himself get into a bus, on his way to a film shoot. As the bus started moving, he felt someone's eyes on him. Turning, he came face-to-face with a transgender dressed in a white kurta-pyjama with the scariest face he had ever seen. 'One look, and I was jolted awake. But I was too frightened to confront the spirit whose presence I could sense in my bedroom,' he shivers at the memory.

When he finally worked up the courage to crack open an eye and look at the clock, he saw that it was exactly 2 a.m. Remembering his aunt's dream, Soham quickly shut his eyes again, terrified out of his wits. As he lay there in that twilight zone, between sleep and wakefulness, the apparition started speaking, 'Tell your father, convince him, that he should fall in with your bua's plans of moving out of that apartment.'

Soham believes that he must have nodded, somewhat uncertainly, his eyes still shut, because the disembodied voice suddenly turned aggressive, rapping out authoritatively, 'Do it... Do it now.'

He waited till he was certain that he was alone again, then sat up, relieved to see that the room was dark and empty. He sneaked a glance at the clock again, it was 2.15 a.m. He broke out in cold sweat. Even if it had been a dream, he had been in the company of the 'visitor' for a quarter of an hour. Then, with the transgender's words, 'Do it... Do it now,' ringing in his ears, he rushed out and headed straight for his parents' bedroom.

When his bemused father opened the door in answer to his frantic knocking, Soham stumbled in, sat on the bed and abruptly told him that he had to immediately tell his sister to move out of that house. 'I was told to tell you this,' he whispered, too frightened to say anything more. Perhaps his father sensed something because instead of plying him with questions, he simply nodded okay and Soham experienced a rush of relief.

Minutes later, he was looking around, wondering what he was doing in his parents' room at that hour. Smiling apologetically, he returned to his own bedroom and almost immediately nodded off. This time, he was not accosted by any unwelcome strangers and slept peacefully for the rest of the night. But when he woke up the next morning, the terror returned. 'It had seemed so real, not like just a dream,' he murmurs.

Shaken, he called his cousin who lived in Ghatkopar and narrated everything to him, urging him to speak to his father too and expedite his aunt's exit from the place. 'He laughed at me, told me that I had gone crazy,' recounts Soham, who wondered what to do next, terrified that the apparition would return if his aunt didn't move out soon.

The next morning, his cousin was back on the line. And this time he wasn't laughing. He sounded as terrified as Soham had been, and almost incoherently, in broken, half sentences, he narrated how he had been woken up late at night by someone who had hauled him out of bed, pushed him roughly against the wall and ordered him to tell his aunt to leave the Kandivali apartment immediately.

'What time did this incident happen?' Soham whispered back. He knew the answer even before his cousin muttered, 'At two in the night.' What surprised him was his cousin's description of his late-night visitor, 'A transgender…dressed in a white kurta-pyjama and a scarf around his neck… And the face was…' As he spoke, Soham realized that it was the exact same face he had seen in his dream, but he had not described it to his cousin the previous day. This meant that he had seen the same person in his dream.

A month after their nightmares, their aunt, with the support of her entire family, including her brother and Soham's father, sold her flat in Kandivali and moved back to her old building. 'She was happy and comfortable there till she passed away a few years later,' says Soham, who never had the dream again.

His cousin, who lives in the US now, has blocked out the memory altogether and refuses to discuss it. No one else in the family has ever spoken about anything like this happening with them. 'But then, we were the only two who had laughed and made fun of my aunt's vision. It's been fifteen years since, but I have not forgotten that face. I never will,' admits the film-maker, who today feels a more empathetic connection with his aunt because a decade later, something similar happened with him.

Around five–six years ago, Soham had rented out a two-bedroom apartment in Juhu which he used as an office. In the year that he worked from there, everything went right with his career and personal life. Tempted, he decided to buy the place even though it meant taking a large loan. Almost immediately, he regretted the decision.

'Earlier, everything I touched had turned to gold. Now, the gold was turning to dust. Even though the flat had been a steal, with deals not coming through and business hitting a rough patch, I was suddenly struggling to pay the high EMIs every month. That year-and-a-half was one of the worst phases in my life when almost everything I did went wrong,' Soham shares.

Three producer-friends who were into vastu shastra told him that a south-facing entrance did not augur well for the residents and urged him to move out. Enquiries revealed that the person from whom he had bought the place had also suffered financial setbacks. And even the one who owned it before that had died prematurely after going bankrupt. 'No one who had bought the place stayed there for longer than three years. The house ruined them and threw them out. Fortunately, with the money I got from the sale of the apartment, I was able to pay back my loan, clear my debts and start afresh. Something is definitely wrong there.'

Soham started his career in advertising. He was brilliant with photoshopping and soon moved to designing film posters. That put him in touch with producer-director Ram Gopal Varma whom he went on to assist on the supernatural horror film *Bhoot* (2003). 'One day, Ramu-ji came to see me at the office. The film was to roll in a month's time and he was going out of town for a few days. In the interim, he wanted me to design a poster and was very categorical that he didn't want the stereotypical *bhootiya* film look. He wanted it to highlight a woman possessed, but he wanted it to look real and natural. It was a big break for an AD (assistant director) and I jumped at the task,' he narrates.

He was neck deep in references when one day, while out jogging, he ran into an old friend, Devang. When he learnt what Soham was doing, Devang suggested a visit to the Mira Datar Dargah located in Reay Road, Mumbai. 'Many of those who are believed to be possessed by a spirit are brought to the dargah to be cured through exorcism. They keep them in chains, I know; my father has been there,' Devang shared.

Soham was instantly excited and, dragging his reluctant friend along, boarded the local train, getting off at the small station which is less than ten minutes away from the city's bustling Chhatrapati Shivaji Terminus and yet a world apart. Stepping out, he spotted a newspaper stall and stopped there to enquire how they could get to the dargah. The vendor looked at Devang and Soham closely, then asked solicitously, '*Sahab, ghar mein sab khairiyat*? (Everyone okay at home?)'

After being assured that all was well, he told them that they could take a bus from outside the station to get to the dargah. 'Why not a taxi?' Soham suggested, and the vendor agreed that taking a cab would make the journey shorter and faster. He rattled off directions and the duo set out to hail a taxi.

'The first one took off like a banshee as soon as the driver heard where we were headed. The second didn't even bother to stop. The third had a Muslim guy at the wheel and I could see him observing us in the rear-view mirror all through the five-minute ride. It was disconcerting,' reminisces Soham.

He dropped them off in front of a narrow bylane saying they would have to walk the rest of the way. 'We heard the voices…people laughing, bawling, screaming…before we saw the dargah where those "possessed by the devil" are brought to be healed by the blessings of Syyed Mira Baba,' says Soham, recalling how on either side of the dingy lane there were shops selling *chadar* (a sheet spread out at the shrine as an offering), holy threads, copies of the Quran, rose water and canopies of flowers.

The dargah was crowded with hundreds of believers, but what caught Soham's eyes were the fifteen to twenty men and women who were sitting, standing, even crawling around on the veranda, making the sounds they had been hearing. 'Their pupils were rolling and some of them were frothing at the mouth, looking almost bestial,' he remembers, admitting that as they passed them on the way to the shrine, they sent a shiver down their backs.

A child who looked to be around twelve or thirteen was doing somersaults, non-stop, unmindful of the cracking sound her bones made. A woman howled like an animal. A man was rolling on the floor and banging his head against the wall. Another was sitting quietly, lost in another world. As Devang cowered against the wall, Soham took out his digicam and started filming, instinctively knowing that his boss, Ram Gopal Varma, would be super excited looking at these pictures.

Inside the dargah, there were normal devotees, some tying holy threads as they made a *mannat*, while others laid out *chadars* in gratitude for a wish fulfilled. Some prayed silently while others sang. 'But what sets this dargah apart, are the ones in chains outside,' he points out.

Soham spent around half-an-hour there, filming the premises, mostly alone, because Devang was too terrified by then to accompany him as he strolled around. He learnt that thousands of people visited the dargah, many with friends and family who were troubled by spirits who had possessed their bodies and turned them violently aggressive. They were brought there every Friday by relatives who believed that Baba, with his powers, would heal them in forty days.

'Suddenly I realized that a *maulvi* was watching me. He didn't say anything, but his eyes were on my camera,' recounts Soham, admitting that he had been furtively capturing the place on film since photography is not allowed. Realizing he had been caught, he slipped him a hundred-rupee note as a token gesture for his silence. '*Beta*, erase whatever you have shot so far. Many TV channels have come here in the past too and filmed the place secretly. The next morning, many of the crew died in an accident,' the maulvi whispered. The words sent a shiver down his back, and Soham instantly did as he was told. Nodding his approval, the maulvi suggested he wait till 7 p.m. and watch the exorcism.

'As the beats of the *nagada* (a huge drum) rent the air, it was as if the demons had come alive. The howls and screams grew louder and more primal, and as the ritual began, the air turned putrid with the smell of vomit,' he shares.

The images imprinted on his mind, Soham returned home and later narrated all that he had seen and heard at the dargah to Ram Gopal Varma. The film-maker was instantly intrigued. The experience helped Soham design some eye-catching posters for *Bhoot*.

He has since been going to the dargah, making at least two visits every year. And has now scripted a web series around it. 'It's a story of what happens to a man in the course of one night,' he informs.

Did anything out of the ordinary happen to him during the shoot of *Bhoot*, you wonder, and Soham laughs. 'Hey, not really, all went well. No supernatural stories there.'

Two years after *Bhoot*, Soham went on to write and direct his own film, *Kaal* (2005). Produced by Karan Johar, whom he assisted on *Kabhi Khushi Kabhie Gham* (2001), and Shah Rukh Khan, the horror thriller is about a battle for survival against supernatural beasts. The story grew out of his many trips to wildlife sanctuaries like the Jim Corbett National Park, the Bandhavgarh National Park and the Kanha Tiger Reserve. 'I always wondered what would happen if I got off the Gypsy while touring the forest and that became the premise for *Kaal*,' he says.

Kaal, despite the cloud of darkness hanging over it, was a smooth shoot without any real-life terrors. But while scripting the web series on the dargah, in a hotel in Matheran, Soham heard many eerie stories from locals there, two of which have inspired another series.

On 4 December 2010, Manish Acharya, who had shot to fame with his debut directorial, the Shabana Azmi-starrer, *Loins of Punjab Presents* (2007), passed away in a freak accident, a day after reaching Matheran. On a holiday with his wife, Dhruvi, and two sons, the forty-year-old film-maker had gone out riding in the morning. The buckle of the saddle snapped and he rolled off the horse. He was not wearing a helmet and suffered a fatal brain hemorrhage. His story is one of Soham's muses.

'I have also incorporated another track revolving around a young mother suffering from postpartum psychosis,' he informs, pointing out that this severe form of mental illness, which starts weeks, even days, after delivering a child, results in the mother blaming everything that is going wrong with her, including weight gain and exhaustion, on the newborn infant. 'Unless treated immediately, it can lead to mania, depression, confusion, delusions and hallucinations, to the extent that she may even try to kill her baby,' Soham warns, adding that his story is a story of a haunting, as scary as the ones he has heard at the Mira Datar Dargah.

11

VISHAL FURIA

Field Day for Horror

Vishal Furia's much-feted directorial debut, *Lapachhapi* (*Hide-and-Seek*, 2017), a Marathi horror film, plays out in a rundown, two-room house, set in the middle of a sugarcane field in rural Maharashtra. The young film-maker had accidentally come across one such field, and after listening to the stories around it, been inspired to spin his own plot, using the field as a metaphor to shed light on the horrific, age-old practice of female infanticide still practiced in our county, resulting in the deaths of three million girls ever year. The story, inspired by true events, and written in just two months, follows a desperate young couple, who flee the city after a run-in with goons, and take shelter in their chauffeur's empty house in the middle of nowhere, only for its dark past to creep up on eight-month pregnant Neha and threaten her unborn child.

The film was shot in just sixteen days in a small village in the interiors of Kolhapur. Walking in the dark, down a path cut through the sugarcane fields, towards the house where all the action was centered, could spook anyone. And when a scream rang out one night, echoing the scream they were filming inside, the unit was disconcerted.

'Turned out that the make-up artist who had been walking towards the house had suddenly pointed at something in the field, screamed loudly, had fallen on her back and fainted. When she was revived, she swore that she had seen a figure dressed in black amidst the swaying stalks,' informs Vishal. Playing the devil's advocate, he reasons that the person who was with the girl had been teasing her about wearing black at night, insisting that it was a colour favoured by the ghosts lurking around. 'This could have brought on the terror fit,' he surmises.

However, having spent the first ten years of his life in Kolhapur, Vishal admits that he has heard many real-life ghost stories from friends and locals who swear that fields like these are definitely haunted. He himself however never experienced anything out of the ordinary when shooting there. He was more focused on the horrors of forced abortions and female feticide that he became aware of through his research and interactions with an NGO. The social evil struck a chord with his largely female audience after the film's release.

'Many women told me that they could empathize with my protagonist Neha because they had gone through something similar themselves or else it had happened to someone they knew,' says Vishal. He recalls one woman in particular who confided that when she was pregnant, they had been living in a high-rise, right behind which there was a gutter. 'She had nightmares every day that buried amidst the sewage were the bodies of young babies who were calling out to her,' he shares.

Finally, to calm her down, her husband called in a paranormal investigator. He didn't find any ghosts there, but he discovered that at the other end of the gutter was a small hospital which was doing illegal sex determination tests. 'Many families don't care for daughters, and when they learnt that it was a female child, they would ask for a termination of the pregnancy. The aborted fetuses were then dumped in the gutter,' the film-maker says.

Vishal's first film has inspired a Hindi remake, *Chhorii (2021)*, with Nushrratt Bharuccha stepping into the shoes of Pooja Sawant to take this little-debated subject to a pan-Indian audience, with the setting changing from rural Maharashtra to north India to increase its reach. *Chhorii* was shot in the midst of the Coronavirus-triggered pandemic, in Madhya Pradesh, and this time, Vishal has no unusual incidents to report. He however had a brush with real-life horror while he was in Goa.

'One night, after a party, I returned to my hotel room around 4 a.m. and promptly fell asleep. A few hours later, I was woken up by the sound of someone knocking on the door,' he reminisces. Vishal opened the door, but to his exasperation, there was no one on the other side. He peered down the corridor and didn't spot anyone. He went back to bed, only to be woken up again by the sound of knocking. This time it was louder and more demanding, coming from inside the washroom. 'I got up groggily, opened the door and once again drew a blank,' he says.

The knocking wouldn't stop, and finally, sleepless and scared, he ran off, leaving his roommate sleeping peacefully. 'When I returned, my roomie was up. I asked him warily if he had heard anyone knocking. He hadn't. I then checked if he had been to the washroom. He had and reported nothing amiss, leaving me wondering if I had really heard something or it was just an illusion brought on by a hangover from drinking too much,' Vishal muses. He however didn't wait to spend another night in that hotel room. They left that evening.

The horror was more real when he arrived at a palace in Baroda to shoot an episode for *Fear Files: Darr Ki Sacchi Tasvirein* (2012–14), a television series hosted by Bipasha Basu. It focuses on different aspects of paranormal activity, from ghosts, zombies and phantoms to witches and wizards. 'That old palace, which had been converted into a hotel, was known to be haunted. A couple of team members did report strange happenings while we were there, like cupboards opening on their own and strident knocking on the door. One girl was spooked when her mobile phone suddenly started playing a song in the middle of the night,' Vishal recounts.

He had been given a suite with a bedroom and a washroom, and a small changing room in between. One night, after a long day of shooting, he returned to the hotel after midnight. Exhausted, Vishal immediately crashed out. He woke up to see the light in the changing room, which he had switched off before going to bed, flickering. He got up and switched off the tubelight, but the flickering continued. 'I wasn't really scared, but I did wonder what was going on. Apart from that light, nothing else happened that night, leaving me thinking that it was flickering because of a faulty electrical connection. It was a really old hotel after all and a spooky place to stay in. But it's a popular location for film shoots, and along with us, there was another film unit staying there at the time.'

Vishal has been fascinated by horror since he was a child, but the Indian movies he saw didn't make much of an impact, unlike their Hollywood counterparts, which when dubbed in Hindi were usually commercially viable. So, he thought of making a film which would change the face of horror in Indian cinema.

He had been working towards an engineering degree, but he quit his studies midway, to work in visual effects for four years. Vishal then moved to broadcasting channels like National Geographic, CNBC, Zee and Sahara as a promo producer and director. After fourteen years in broadcasting, he entered the industry, wanting to make a feature film.

He wrote *Lapachhapi*, struggled for over a year to find a producer who didn't want him to spice up his script with sex and songs and thereby dilute the horror, a common mistake with Indian cinema. Businessman-turned-producer Jitendra Patil gave him the leeway to make the film honestly and authentically. Releasing it was another struggle. Vishal's perseverance finally paid off and the film went on to win awards and accolades.

He then co-directed eight episodes of the television series *Criminal Justice* (2019), the sports television drama *Bombers* (2019–20) and five episodes of the series *The Missing Stone* (2020). In November 2019, when lockdown restrictions brought on by the pandemic were lifted, Vishal rolled with his second feature film, with Swapnil Joshi, Pooja Sawant and Pritam Kagne. *Bali* (2021) was completed in February 2021. Another Marathi horror film, it revolves around a widowed father and his seven-year-old son, who suddenly collapses and is rushed to hospital. While he is undergoing treatment there, the little boy starts talking to a mysterious nurse who, he claims, stays in an abandoned wing of the hospital.

'We shot a portion of the film in Pune's Deccan College. When we were on a recce there, I was looking up at the windows because in a particular scene, I needed one of my characters to look out of one. As I pointed out one of the windows to my DoP, Rajan Sohani, it suddenly opened on its own,' Vishal recounts.

It was disconcerting because there wasn't a strong breeze blowing that day. Nor was anyone looking down at them. They moved to another part of the college, and once again, when Vishal pointed to a window, it opened. 'The college has hundreds of windows, many of which were shuttered that day. Only the ones I was pointing to would open. I cracked a joke, saying the ghosts were inviting us in, like we welcome guests. Well, if they were, they didn't trouble us during the shoot unlike what happens on screen,' he concludes with a smile.

12

ASHOK KUMAR

Murder and a Mahal

Ashok Kumar had always loved stories. But more than listening to them, he enjoyed weaving stories of his own. During his school vacations, he would visit his maternal grandfather in Bhagalpur, a wealthy philanthropist who shared his passion for stories.

It was there that the thirteen-year-old Ashok Kumar met a young writer, who was urged on by his grandfather to sit with the boy every evening on the veranda of their house and tell him a story.

'I would soon get bored of listening to him and after interrupting him with several questions, would end up telling him my story,' the actor recounted. After a few days, the writer went to his grandfather complaining that Kumud (he was christened Kumudlal Ganguly by his parents and given the screen name Ashok Kumar by his mentor) didn't allow him to talk.

Seventeen years later, in 1938, Ashok Kumar, now a top star, arrived in New Theatres Studio in Calcutta (now Kolkata) to shoot for a film. He was greeted warmly by several bigwigs, including director Nitin Bose, singer, actor and composer

Pankaj Mullick and famous Bengali litterateur Sarat Chandra Chatterjee. When he was introduced to Chatterjee, the author of *Srikanto*, *Devdas* and *Parineeta* (which Ashok Kumar later adapted into films), smiled and wondered if the actor would like to tell him a story. Noticing his bemused expression, his favourite novelist reminded him of their early meetings in Bhagalpur. 'Imagine, I had been telling my stories to none other than Sarat babu,' Dadamoni, as he came to be fondly called, had guffawed, in an interview to Junior G, edited by Bhawana Somaaya.

I once asked Ashok Kumar to tell me one of his tales, but one that had happened in real. He narrated how one night, in the 1940s, while staying at Khandala's Jeejeebhoy House, he was alerted by some commotion outside. Stepping out, he had spotted a young lady by the gate of the bungalow, arguing heatedly with a man. It turned out that he was her chauffeur, and she was livid because their car had broken down at that late hour in a secluded place. Dadamoni courteously invited her to wait with him inside, telling the chauffeur to call her once he had fixed the problem. They were chatting amicably when the chauffeur knocked on the door. He admitted he was unable to figure out the problem with the car and was afraid they would have to spend the night there.

Instantly, the lady's temper flared and, turning down Dadamoni's invitation to stay in the bungalow that night, she stormed out, the chauffeur at her heels. He shut the door after them and went to bed, but was woken up soon after by someone screaming for help. Once again, he stepped out to hear cries of help coming from inside the parked car.

He hurried across, peered in through the window and got the shock of his life! The chauffeur, his throat cut, was at the wheel. And even as he watched in horror, the man breathed his last. The woman was nowhere to be seen. Dadamoni ran back to the safety of the bungalow and locked himself in.

The next morning, after a long and sleepless night, he went to the local police station with the property's caretaker to file an FIR for murder. The car and the corpse had mysteriously disappeared, but he was able to give a clear description of the duo and what had transpired, which, he presumed, had cost the chauffeur his life. The inspector on duty was not surprised by what he narrated and after listening to him patiently, told Dadamoni that fourteen years ago, a young woman had cut a man's throat after an altercation. She had left the dying man in the car that had been parked just outside Jeejeebhoy House and had fled the crime scene. She, however, didn't go too far, as she was soon killed in an accident. Since then, he admitted, there had been reports, on and off, of paranormal activity around the building.

Dadamoni returned to Jeejeebhoy House wondering if he had seen ghosts. He never forgot that night.

In 1947, he bought Bombay Talkies Studio, where he had started his career. He was saddled with pending debts amounting to Rs 28 lakh, but the success of *Majboor* (1948) helped him clear them. However, the films that followed didn't succeed commercially, and Dadamoni knew they would have to come up with a blockbuster to keep the studio going. That's when Kamal Amrohi, one of the most sought-after writers of the time, came to Bombay Talkies with a story he had written. The story immediately sparked the interest of Dadamoni's production partner, Savak Wacha.

The story revolved around the aristocratic Hari Shankar, who is drawn to a foreboding *mahal.* Inside, he stumbles upon a framed picture of a man who bears a striking resemblance to him. He learns from the property's gardener that it is the portrait of a man who used to come to the mahal to meet the girl he loved but couldn't marry. Then, one day, he had just disappeared.

The gardener's daughter, Kamini, in her desperation to escape her life of drudgery and poverty, decides to use the story to manipulate Hari Shankar into marrying her. She soon has him under her spell, convincing him that he was that man in another life and she the girl he had lost. His obsession with a 'ghost' eventually drives his wife to suicide and puts him in the dock.

Savak Wacha wanted to buy the rights of the story. But Kamal Amrohi refused to part with them unless they let him direct the film. Unwilling to bet on a debutant director when the studio was going through a bad patch, Wacha told him he would need to consult his partner. When he sounded him out, Dadamoni suggested they offer Amrohi double. But money was not a priority with the man who was already among the highest paid writers then. He wanted to direct movies and told Wacha that he was ready to cut his fee by half if given the opportunity.

'Sign him then, since he is so determined,' Dadamoni decided, and even gambled with a little-known, sixteen-year-old actress, who was half his age. The film, *Mahal* (1949), launched not just Kamal Amrohi's career as a director, but also made its leading lady Madhubala and playback singer Lata Mangeshkar household names. '*Aayega Aanewala*' still haunts us, the way the eerie encounter at Jeejeebhoy had haunted Dadamoni.

13

PREM SAGAR

Message from a Ouija Board

Prem Sagar will never forget going to The Royal Opera House in Mumbai with his father Ramanand Sagar—acclaimed writer, producer, and director—for the first day, first show of their home production *Bazooband* (1954). Featuring Balraj Sahni and Sulochana Chatterjee in the lead, the film was a tussle for supremacy between virtue and vice. 'We were expecting a full house, but to our shock, not a single ticket was sold. Imagine just two people in an entire movie hall. I had never seen anything like this before or since,' the film-maker recalls.

Ramanand Sagar had been riding high after the commercial success of Raj Kapoor's *Barsaat* (1949) and Dilip Kumar's *Sangdil* (1952), both written by him. But this disaster coming on the heels of his debut directorial, *Mehmaan* (1953), written by him and produced under his banner Sagar Arts (set up in 1950 with composer Anil Biswas and his wife Asha), meant that he was suddenly without work. During this period, the family had to survive by selling dried melon seeds.

Then, out of the blue, Maulana Abul Kalam Azad, India's first Education Minister, approached him.

'Maulana sahab had worked in a newspaper (*The Vakil*), set up Urdu weekly newspapers (*Al-Hilal and Al-Balagh*), and written many books, including *India Wins Freedom*. He knew papaji from the forties, had read his books and respected him. Maulana sahab wanted papaji to join a group of writers and intellectuals on a three-month literary tour across the country. On their return, their literary works were to reflect all that they had seen and experienced,' informs Prem Sagar.

It was too good an opportunity to miss, given that it was a fully paid trip, yet Ramanand Sagar was reluctant. How would his family, including his six children, sustain themselves with him gone for three months? 'In a dilemma, papaji set out his Ouija board and lit a candle. He had got into the habit of communicating with spirits and the one he summoned that evening, in answer to his question, 'Should I go?' replied decisively, 'Yes.' Papaji still demurred, wondering how his family would manage once he was gone. But every time he put forward a query regarding the trip, the only answer he got from the spirit was a 'yes'. Eventually, he decided to board the train, hoping the journey would bring him some work,' recounts his cinematographer–film-maker son.

Once the decision was made, the family rallied around Ramanand Sagar. His wife, Leelavati, handed him hundred rupees in loose coins that she had managed to save from household expenses. One of the children broke his piggy bank and another offered a hoarded apple as the writer–film-maker set off for the railway station the next morning. The three months passed by in a flash. At every stop, he met many like-minded people and made several friends. The journey was exhilarating, but with no film offers forthcoming, worry sat heavily on his shoulders.

The last stop was Madras (now Chennai), where they were to visit the Bharatiya Vidya Bhavan. At the station, he met a man who had been sent to escort him to Gemini Studios, one of the biggest production houses at the time, with its own labs and distribution network. Ramanand Sagar was pleasantly surprised, more so when in the car he learnt that his escort, dressed simply in a white *mundu-kurta,* was none other than the studio's big boss and famous film-maker SS Vasan. 'He had been reading papaji's books since 1942, including *Maut Ke Bistar Se* (*Diary of a TB Patient*), and wanted him to join the studio permanently,' informs Prem Sagar.

The association was fruitful and produced several big hits, starting with *Insaniyat* (1955), which Ramanand Sagar not only wrote for the studio, but also got Dilip Kumar, Dev Anand and Bina Rai on board. He then went on to pen the Gemini Ganesan and Vyjayanthimala starrer *Raj Tilak* (1959), and *Paigham* (1959), in which Dilip Kumar and Raaj Kumar play warring brothers. A year later, he directed *Ghunghat* (1960), followed by *Zindagi* (1964), *Arzoo* (1965) and *Aankhen* (1968), and there was no looking back. To this day, his family remains eternally grateful to the spirit that had urged him to grab the opportunity when he was dithering. 'Had it not been for that message from the Ouija board, papaji may not have made the trip,' acknowledges Prem Sagar who has penned a book tracing his father's journey, *An Epic Life: Ramanand Sagar: From Barsaat to Ramayan,* published by Penguin.

A decade later, Ramanand Sagar was shooting *Charas* (1976), a film revolving around narcotics smuggling, with Amjad Khan playing the kingpin who operates from his cave-like den in Malta, a tiny island in the middle of the Mediterranean Sea. They had set up a huge set in Mumbai's Natraj Studio and surrounded it with one lakh fifty thousand gallons of water. Inside the cave was a small landing to the left of which was a bridge at a height of about forty feet, which connected both sides of the cave. One day, Prem Sagar, who was the film's cinematographer, was standing on the bridge with four others when the base gave way.

'When he saw us, papaji, his heart in his mouth, whispered, "Are they still breathing?" Two of the unit members had died, but I had survived the fall. I tried to stand but couldn't. I couldn't even move. Mansoor *bhai*, one of the stuntmen, swung from a rope like Tarzan and jumped to our rescue,' he reminisces.

Prem Sagar broke sixteen bones in that fall and had to spend a year in hospital. He lost hearing in his left ear, but he is grateful that he isn't confined to a wheelchair and can still work ten-twelve hours a day. However, before he could get back on his feet, he had an out-of-body experience that still sends shivers down his spine.

'One day, while I was lying in bed, surrounded by my family, I suddenly felt I was standing in the corner of the room, watching myself die. In blind panic, I called out to my parents, brothers, wife and children, urging them to save me. But though I was shouting at the top of my voice, they couldn't hear me. I then directed my efforts towards re-entering my inert body. After a few minutes, I succeeded and sat up in bed, weeping profusely, much to the shock of my family,' Prem Sagar recalls.

To this day he is unable to logically explain the incident. He believes that his soul departed his body. 'But maybe it was not time for me to die yet, so I returned to the living to complete my *putra dharma* (son's duty) and my *pitra-rin* (parental debt) and take my father's legacy forward. Or maybe it was my parents' prayers and their karma that extended my lifespan? Whatever the reason, for a few minutes there, I was dead, and I knew it too,' he concludes.

14

SHAKTI SAMANTA

In My Footsteps...

He was not someone you would associate with horror films. The name Shakti Samanta brings back memories of a sexy Madhubala grooving to '*Aaiye Meherbaan*' in *Howrah Bridge* (1958), Shammi Kapoor serenading Sharmila Tagore from the skies in *An Evening in Paris* (1967) and Rajesh Khanna saying 'Pushpa, I hate tears,' with that heart-stopping half smile in *Amar Prem* (1972). He directed thirty-seven films in Hindi, six in Bengali and produced twelve more, most of them directed by his son Ashim, in a career spanning almost five decades. He made films in a variety of genres—from crime thrillers to musicals, from social dramas to rom coms—with effortless ease. But he never tried his hand at horror, perhaps because of a particular incident during his early days in Mumbai.

After graduating from Calcutta University in 1944, Shakti *da*, as he was fondly known in the Bollywood fraternity, came to Bombay (now Mumbai) to become an actor and a singer. Ashok Kumar advised him to become a director instead, so in the late 1940s, he became an assistant director.

He had rented a room in Andheri's Seven Bungalows which was not the booming suburb it is today, packed with houses and the lanes bustling with traffic. Back then, the area used to be quite deserted, particularly late at night. Samanta, then in his early twenties, used to return home quite late. He would get off at Andheri station and walk home, since money was in short supply and transport was hard to find at that hour.

It was almost an hour's walk and, on the way, Samanta passed by the Shai Imami Ismaili Muslim Kabristan, close to the Four Bungalows market. At that hour, the area around the cemetery can send shivers down the spine even today. Spooky stories usually accompany burial grounds, but this kabristan never featured in the list of Mumbai's haunted places. However, Ashim recounts how his father was frightened out of his wits one night passing by the cemetery.

'On his way back home, dad sensed an eerie shadow behind him and turned around to see whether he was being followed. He didn't see anyone or hear any footsteps, so he continued walking. But he felt a presence, so he quickened his pace. From the corner of his eye, he could still see the dark shadow following him. Petrified, he looked over his shoulder, wondering if he was merely frightened of his own shadow. But it wasn't his,' recounts Ashim, admitting that till his last day, his father, who had made so many mystery movies, was unable to solve this one mystery.

'That night, he simply shut his eyes and ran all the way home, muttering "Ram Ram",' Ashim concludes.

15

RANJEETA KAUR

Floating Djinn of Worli

She has been away from the studio arc lights for a while now, but even after four decades, one still remembers Ranjeeta Kaur from her debut film *Laila Majnu* (1976), Harman Singh Rawail's tragic romance. Entreating a gathering in a marketplace to not pelt stones at her lover, she croons, '*Husn haazir hai, mohabbat ki sazaa paane ko, koi patthar se na maare mere deewane ko.*' Clinging to Rishi Kapoor's Majnu at the end of the song, her kohl-streaked eyes wide with terror, Ranjeeta became the darling of a nation that never tires of this timeless love story. She went on to have an impressive career for over a decade, with hits such as *Pati Patni Aur Woh* (1978), *Ankhiyon Ke Jharokhon Se* (1978), *Surakksha* (1979), *Taqdeer Ka Badshah* (1981) and *Satte Pe Satta* (1982), before she bowed out, opting for marriage and motherhood over showbiz.

Even today, she remembers an incident from her first film. 'I had recently graduated from the Film and Television Institute of India (FTII) and was staying with my sister while shooting for *Laila Majnu*, since I didn't have a place of my own. One night, I woke up with a start to find myself staring at a middle-aged man, who had one foot on my bed and the other on the floor,' she narrates.

For a minute or two Ranjeeta wondered if she was dreaming, then turned cold when she realized he *was* standing there in front of her. Dressed in a suit and a hat, a cigar clenched between his teeth, he seemed from another world and time. 'I was quite young at the time and was terrified as I stared at him. Thankfully, he left soon after. I thank my stars he didn't hurt me. Talking about the incident still gives me gooseflesh,' admits the actress.

Fortunately for Ranjeeta, her sister was already planning to move out of the apartment, so she didn't have to worry about spending too many nights there. 'A woman who wanted to buy the apartment had brought along someone who could feel the presence of spirits. This person told her she was not getting good vibes from it. Subsequently, we learnt that a woman had been shot there,' she recollects.

There was another spooky incident she experienced. She was out with some friends from FTII, including Vikram Sahu, actor Kishore Sahu's son, who is still remembered as *Satte Pe Satta*'s Shukra. 'We were going to the Taj Mahal Hotel to drop off a friend's friend. It was a little past midnight and we were in Worli, driving past a movie theatre. The night show had just ended and people were streaming out,' Ranjeeta recalls.

A man, running like a maniac, unmindful of the traffic, suddenly cut across the street. Braking to a stop, they called out to him angrily. Still running for his life, he panted, '*Woh mere peeche hai* (She's after me),' and disappeared down the road. What happened next still gives Ranjeeta the shivers when she is alone. 'Suddenly, a figure appeared, floating several feet above the ground. Dressed in a long, black, flowing robe, and a Bedouin-style face mask, commonly used by Arab women, the figure was chasing the man. Then, much to our shock, it turned and vanished into the sea,' she remembers, admitting that it's a story that she would not have believed had she not seen it with her own eyes, along with several others who will corroborate it.

They continued with their drive, but the memory stayed with her. A couple of years later, it cropped up again when a spot boy, who used to stay near actor Raaj Kumar's sea-facing bungalow in Worli, happened to mention the djinn who lived near the *kachre ka dabba* (dustbin) in the area. 'His description matched the figure we had seen that night, so maybe it was the djinn,' Ranjeeta muses.

When asked if she believes in spirits, she states emphatically, 'Oh yes, they exist, two hundred per cent. And like humans, there are good and bad spirits. The man I saw in the flat did not mean any harm, but the floating figure in Worli was definitely evil,' she pronounces.

When Ranjeeta was in Ooty for a shoot, with Saroj Khan and her troupe, they were staying at Fern Hill Hotel, which back then had a reputation for being haunted. She barely slept the first night she checked in. 'Around 3 a.m., I was woken up by the sound of water dripping; I went into the bathroom to find that the bathtub tap was open. Initially, I thought it was a plumbing issue, so I turned it off and went back to bed. But minutes later, water started dripping again. The tap had turned itself on automatically. This time I freaked out and changed my room immediately,' she says, adding that later, the hotel staff admitted that the room was haunted by a woman's spirit.

16

B SUBHASH

Something White in the Night

His first production, *Disco Dancer* (1982), was a surprise blockbuster that also went on to become a cult film. Babbar Subhash's film had introduced disco to India and made its hero, Mithun Chakraborty, a demigod in Bollywood. The musical drama was equally popular across continents—Southern, Central and Eastern Asia, Europe and Africa. It also had people in Eastern Europe, in particular Russia, dancing to the tunes of '*Jimmy jimmy aaja aaja*'.

Buoyed by its success, towards the end of the eighties, producer-director Babbar Subhash decided to remake the film. He sounded out Uganda-based businessman Kirit Trivedi, a friend of Amitabh Bachchan, and the pioneer of Indian concerts abroad. Trivedi loved the idea and introduced him to a British Lord who was happy to come on board as the producer.

'I worked on the project for two–three years, flying out to London several times to learn how the film industry worked there. Unfortunately, the Lord suffered a huge financial loss all of a sudden and pulled out,' recalls

Subhash, who even two decades later hoped to take *Disco Dancer* to Hollywood.

Back in the eighties and early nineties, he went on to make more hits, like the musical revenge-drama *Kasam Paida Karne Wale Ki* (1984) and the action-packed *Aandhi-Toofan* (1985). There was also the fantasy romance, *Adventures of Tarzan* (1985), followed by *Dance Dance* (1987), *Commando* (1988), *Love Love Love* (1989), *Aaj Ke Angaarey* (1988) and *Pyaar Ke Naam Qurbaan* (1990).

Towards the end of the nineties, B Subhash revived his dream of making an English film with a Hollywood actor and launched the reincarnation drama, *Divine Lovers* (1997), which featured Maxwell Caulfield from *Grease 2* (1982), an American-Irish actress Shannon McLeod, and his 'Tarzan', Hemant Birje.

'During my stay in London and Los Angeles, I had learnt that people there primarily liked three places in India—Rajasthan, Agra and Khajuraho, with a few making a trip to Varanasi too. Since we had seen the palaces of Jaipur and the Taj Mahal in many films, I decided to plot a film inspired by the Khajuraho temples. The books I had read on Khajuraho intrigued me because there are these erotic sculptures carved on the outside walls of the temples which house a shrine inside,' says Subhash.

He wove a story around a fictitious American architect, Jeff Thompson, played by Maxwell, who is plagued by nightmares of a sculptor killing him. On his visit to India, he meets Reeta, enacted by Shannon, the wife of a wealthy and womanizing royal, Prince Kabir, played by Marc Zuber. They fall in love, and one day, while on a visit to an archaeological site, realize that the reason they had been instantly drawn to each other was because they are the reincarnated avatars of Urvashi and Chandra, lovers in their previous life. Urvashi had been forced by the sculptor Gregory to pose nude with Chandra in an excavated cave, where the lovers had consummated their relationship. An enraged Gregory had hit Chandra on the head with a hammer and left his body in the cave, where it had been consumed by flames, while the sculptor had run away with Urvashi.

Reunited in this birth, they grow closer, only to be interrupted by him, who is the reincarnated sculptor. They manage to kill him, but then an earthquake seals them in the cave. The divine lovers surrender to another untimely end, promising each other that their love will never die.

For the most part, the film was shot in a cave constructed on one of the two stages in the Film and Television Institute of India (FTII). Interestingly, the set had first been built in Mumbai's RK Studio, but after shooting was halted in the city following a flash strike, it was transported to Pune on a truck in parts and reconstructed.

From there they flew to Jaipur, then to the Hogenakkal Falls, continuing on to Khajuraho. En route, they had a brief stopover in Agra, and as their flight was delayed, Maxwell cajoled Subhash for a quick visit to the Taj Mahal. The American actor had signed the film on the condition that he would be taken to Jaipur and Agra. After visiting the Taj Mahal, they hurried back to the airport, where they saw the plane taking off with some of their crew and luggage, as the disgruntled pilot had refused to wait for them.

Unwilling to waste a day in Agra twiddling his thumbs with the American actors, Subhash, with their consent, decided to take a train to Gwalior. From there they would drive down to Khajuraho, so they could reach by midnight and start shooting early the next morning. On the way to the temple town, they persuaded the driver to stop for tea and *pakoras* (fritters) at a roadside *dhaba a*round 11 p.m., as they were chilled to the bone. The driver was reluctant, warning them that the area was notorious for dacoits, but they insisted and woke up the dhaba owner, persuading him to prepare some snacks and tea for them.

'It was only after we had left the dhaba that the driver quietly told me that he had seen dacoits come out of the shadows and stride towards us purposefully. But then, noticing the Americans, they had changed their plans, unwilling to loot *firangs* (foreigners) and give our country a bad name,' the film-maker narrates, adding that for him, the shoot of *Divine Lovers* is unforgettable for this close shave with the notorious bandits of Madhya Pradesh.

When asked whether he believes in reincarnation, Subhash admits that *Divine Lovers* was just a story. 'But I do believe in karma,' he is quick to add.

What about spirits? He confides that while he has not had any paranormal experience, some of his crew members did. While they were shooting near the majestic Hogenakkal Waterfalls, on the border of Tamil Nadu's Dharmapuri district and the Chamarajanagar district of Karnataka, some of his unit had stepped out one night. When they returned to the small government hotel where they were staying, they were scared out of their wits. 'They claimed they had seen white clothes floating in the air, which they believed were ghosts. I laughed and told them that it must be someone's laundry blown away by the wind and was ready to go and see this strange phenomenon for myself, but they wouldn't let me go. Later, some locals confirmed their story, insisting that ghosts wandered around the vicinity of the hotel in the dark,' Subhash recounts, admitting that the hotel where they were staying was like a haunted house.

17

ARUNARAJE PATIL

A Message from My Daughter

When you think of horror in Hindi cinema, a film that instantly comes to mind is Arunaraje Patil and Vikas Desai's *Gehrayee* (1980). The horror-thriller revolves around a young girl, Uma, who pays the price for her father's decision to sell his plantation to a factory. Chennabasappa, who is living in Bangalore (now Bengaluru) and is heading a business company, sells his farms and land in his ancestral village. This enrages Baswa, the plantation's caretaker, who considers it an act of betrayal to the land. One day, Uma starts behaving strangely and as her condition worsens, some unspeakable chapters from her father's dark past come to the fore.

Finally, it is revealed that Baswa had paid a local tantrik to send a demonic spirit to possess Uma, the spell cast by a lemon and a voodoo doll. After an exorcism, the young girl returns to normal, but her brother, Nandu, confronts the caretaker's soul to learn why he put Uma through such hell. The spirit doesn't spare him either.

It was Aruna's idea to make a truly terrifying horror film. She got the inspiration while shooting for *Shaque* (1976)—

featuring Vinod Khanna and Shabana Azmi—along with Vikas, her then husband and co-director.

The National Award winner says that when she was ten, her family—parents, two sisters and two brothers—had moved to Bangalore. 'We lived in a bungalow with a huge garden. My mother loved gardening and was always pottering around, while I would climb trees and sit on the branches,' Aruna reminisces with a laugh.

Things were great until lemons smeared with *kumkum* (vermillion) and *haldi* (turmeric powder) were found lying around or buried in the garden. 'My father was in politics and there was talk of jealous rivals and opponent party workers resorting to black magic to cast spells on us. My mother would get really upset when she came across these lemons and would burn them in a bonfire. My grandmother would spit on them and chant a mantra. I was too young to understand much, but their anger and fear stayed with me,' the writer-director recounts.

Gehrayee has its roots in Aruna's early memories. The film took Vikas and her on a journey into a dark world that they had been clueless about till then. For research, they met several practitioners of black magic and some of the victims, heard stories of possession and *yantra-tantra* induced submission of the body. Soon Vikas was as excited as her about diving into this largely untapped genre. However, it wasn't till *The Exorcist* (1971) became the highest grossing R-rated horror film—a record broken only forty-four years later in 2017 by *It*—and the first horror film to be nominated for a Best Picture Oscar, that their *Shaque* producer, N.B. Kamat, agreed to co-produce the film with Vikas.

Like *Gehryaee*, *The Exorcist* too had revolved around the demonic possession of a schoolgirl. Aruna has often been asked if she believes in possession. She says she's not sure, but has heard first-person accounts of people who have had to deal with it. A well-known writer had told them about her sixteen-year-old sister who was possessed while returning from college when she stepped on the remains of a puja under a tree.

In her memoir, *Freedom, My Story*, published by HarperCollins, Aruna writes about how that very evening, the young girl underwent startling changes, beginning to speak chaste Urdu in a cultured male voice as the spirit that had possessed her had been a professor in Lucknow who had died in a train accident. 'When the professor realized that her family was finding it difficult to follow what he was saying through her, he began teaching them Urdu too,' narrates Aruna.

But while the spirit was always courteous with her family, it would often physically torture the girl at night. Unable to see her in so much pain, the family turned to exorcists for help, but it was difficult to dislodge 'the professor'. Meanwhile, the possessed girl was growing alarmingly emaciated despite gorging on huge amounts of biryani. Tests revealed she had hardly eaten in months and her intestines had shrunk. Scared of losing her, the family set off to the Sri Dattatreya Temple in Ganagapur. They stayed in Karnataka for weeks, living off the alms of devotees. Unable to enter the temple, the spirit eventually left the girl's body. 'And she effortlessly slipped back into the life she had led before the possession, with absolutely no recollection of what had transpired, getting married the following year. Her sister, however, continued to speak chaste Urdu, even spouting *sher-shayari* on occasions,' the film-maker recalls.

Aruna was privy to another case of possession, involving a boy who was the same age as her siblings and her and they had met a few times with the family. One day, he met with an accident and was rushed to Vani Vilas Hospital in Bangalore. 'Since all the beds and stretchers were occupied, one of the staff members set a corpse down on the floor so they could place the boy on a table. When he regained consciousness, he was speaking in fluent Tamil, a language he hadn't known,' she recounts.

The boy told his bewildered family that he had been injured in a bus accident and was worried his wife and children would get anxious when he didn't return home. Eventually, they figured that he had been possessed by the spirit of the dead man who had been lying on the table. They reached out to their Catholic priest who tried to exorcize the spirit, and on failing, instructed them to go to the small town in Tamil Nadu where the man had lived and convey the news of his untimely demise to his family. 'Only after that the spirit was finally at peace and left the boy's body. The child had no memory of what had happened and went back to his normal life,' she informs.

Aruna goes on to share that a similar case happened in her own home. One night, when noted playwright Vijay Tendulkar, Vikas and she were working on the script of *Gehrayee*, they were alerted by raised voices coming from the kitchen. She got up to investigate and found their young maid rolling on the floor, shaking, weeping and babbling incoherently.

While Aruna and Vikas were clueless about how to deal with the girl, the male servants got into action. 'Initially, they told us that she was having a fit and made her sniff onions. After a while, she calmed down, but now the help was convinced it was a case of possession,' she says.

Gehrayee is still remembered for Padmini Kolhapure's spine-chilling performance as the possessed Uma, along with Amrish Puri's evil tantric who wants to deflower the virginal teenager to increase his own powers. 'I had learnt of *vashikaran* (love spell) during our research. That's what Puttachary uses to make Uma submit to him. Fortunately, he is thwarted at the last moment by her brother,' points out the director.

Amrish Puri had revealed that Steven Spielberg was so impressed by his portrayal in *Gehrayee* that he got called to an audition in Bombay (now Mumbai). He was handed a full page of dialogue written in English and was asked to memorize his lines in ten minutes. The actor told the casting director that was 'impossible' and on camera, spoke a lot of gibberish. His improvisations and his powerful acting landed him the much-coveted role of the evil priest Mola Ram in the blockbuster Hollywood movie, *Indiana Jones and the Temple of Doom* (1984).

Meanwhile, *Gehrayee* continued to make waves.

'Vikas and I had been warned against dabbling with the occult, and though we did not take the warning seriously then, within a few years, we had lost our nine-year-old daughter Gaagi. Subsequently, my marriage fell apart and our once happy family was destroyed forever,' admits Aruna.

Gaagi had been diagnosed with bone cancer while she was shooting for her parents' film, *Situm* (1982). They rushed her to the US where her leg was operated upon. She returned home after a triumphant surgery, having won the first battle over cancer. 'But the malaise returned, and eventually, her leg had to be amputated. It didn't stop the cancer from spreading and taking her away,' shares her heartbroken mother.

Before her death, Gaagi had promised Aruna that she would come back and meet her. So, after her death, for a while, the distraught mother, believing that her Gaagi would return, would look at little girls and wonder if one of them was her daughter. 'But eventually, I accepted that Gaagi was gone and she wasn't coming back,' she says.

Aruna was still disturbed when she ran into Shiamak Davar at the Willingdon Club. The choreographer, who had known about Gaagi's demise, persuaded her to meet Khorshed Bhavnagri. He informed that the author too had lost both her sons when they were very young and had learnt automatic writing to communicate with them. Shiamak, who practices psychography himself, was sure she would put Aruna in touch with Gaagi too.

The film-maker admits that she was reluctant to go and had thought of declining till the last minute. But eventually, she allowed herself to be persuaded. Despite Khorshed's attempts, however, Aruna wasn't able to connect with Gaagi. 'I guess, I was both resistant and reluctant to make contact. It had been difficult, but by then, I had made peace with the fact that no matter how much I wanted, I wasn't going to get my Gaagi back. My daughter was gone and I didn't want to pull her back from the world she was in now,' she reasons. 'So, I simply wrote "Love you darling" many times and left.'

Aruna then tried different kinds of meditation to gain the strength to move forward. On the face of it, she was strong and independent, made films, but just below the surface, she felt a lot of agony as she continued looking for answers. 'Much later, another gentleman, a foreigner who could communicate with spirits, got in touch, saying he wanted to ask a couple of questions,' she shares.

During a séance, he informed that he had seen an elderly lady with her head covered who was concerned for her. He wanted to know how Aruna was related to her. 'From his description, I surmised that she was my grandmother who had passed away long ago,' says the film-maker.

Then, he told her that a child wanted him to pass on a message to her mother. 'Intrigued, I asked him what the message was. He said she had told him to tell me she was "whole and complete" again. He was puzzled by the message, but I understood perfectly. Those words finally gave me the peace I had been seeking. I had seen for myself how much pain Gaagi had been in when her leg was amputated and how hard it was for her to deal with the loss of a limb. To know that she was whole and complete again gave me the strength to get on with my own life,' Aruna asserts.

Over the years, many have asked her if given a chance to turn the clock back, would she have preferred not having Gaagi and going through months of hopeless and helpless agony, watching her young daughter waste away and finally leave her. Her answer to that query has always been, 'No, I would go through it, again and again, because Gaagi brought me so much joy. She taught me many important lessons and how to cope with life.' But, Aruna adds, at the same time, it is nice to know that her daughter is well and whole in another world, free of all pain and still thinking of her mother.

18

DIVYA DUTTA

The Ultimatum

In the late nineties, Divya Dutta was at a crucial crossroads of her life. 'I was in a dilemma: Should I keep making rounds of producers' offices only to be politely told that they had nothing substantial and take whatever offers come my way? Or should I return home to Ludhiana and look for other career options, even though my heart lies in acting? I was getting roles in films, but they were mostly in multi-starrers and not the kind of work I wanted to do,' shares the actress, who had come to Mumbai to take part in the Stardust talent hunt contest. She sailed through the auditions and was launched with six others in the film *Ishq Mein Jeena Ishq Mein Marna* (1994).

However, after a year of living alone in Mumbai, Divya's steely resolve to make a place for herself in the film industry was beginning to crumble. What made it worse was that there was no one she could pour her heart out to. She knew if she confided in her mother, Dr Nalini, she would immediately book her the next flight home or leave everything and come there to be with her. 'With no one else to talk to, I started venting to the huge picture of Shirdi's Sai Baba in my room.

I spoke to Baba as if he were my parent, telling him between sobs that I couldn't go on this way. I felt defeated. Then, *rooth ke* (sulkily), I gave him an ultimatum. He had one day to change the course of my career, failing which I would return home for good,' the actress reminisces.

She had not expected any miracle to happen within twenty-four hours, but the very next day, writer Sanjay Chhel called to inform her that Pamela Rooks wanted to meet her. Rooks was making a film on Khushwant Singh's 1956 novel, *Train to Pakistan,* and she had Divya in mind for a role. Divya was delighted. The journalist-turned-film-maker's first feature, *Miss Beatty's Children* (1992), based on her novel by the same name, had bagged her the Indira Gandhi Award for Best Debut Film of a Director at the National Film Awards. Could this be the break she had been waiting for?

'The same evening, I went to meet Pamela with several of my glamorous pictures, because that's what everyone wanted to see back then. She took one look at the pictures and told me quite frankly that she didn't like them. My heart sank, and I launched into an internal monologue about booking a ticket for home, when she surprised me by saying she liked the way I looked in person and my childlike innocence and wanted to cast me as the Muslim prostitute Haseena, one of the leads. Before the day had ended, I had landed the role and a film of my dreams,' Divya recounts. *Train to Pakistan* (1998) was the turning point in her career.

The following year, she made her debut in Punjabi cinema with *Shaheed-e-Mohabbat Boota Singh* (1999). Based on a tragic real life love story, it features Gurdas Mann as Boota Singh, a former Sikh soldier, and Divya as Zainab, the Muslim girl he marries and who is forcibly deported to Pakistan after the Partition. Produced under Mann's banner by his wife Manjeet, it was the toast of the national and international festival circuit and was adjudged Best Feature Film in Punjabi by the National Award jury.

After that, there was no looking back. With Shyam Benegal's *Samar* (1999) and *Welcome to Sajjanpur* (2008), Yash Chopra's *Veer-Zaara* (2004), Rakeysh Om Prakash Mehra's *Delhi-6* (2009) and *Bhaag Milkha Bhaag* (2013), Divya established herself as a powerhouse of talent. Today, she is the proud recipient of the National Award for Best Supporting Actress for the social drama *Irada* (2017).

'That day, Baba blessed me. He carved my destiny before I could pack my bags and gave my career the direction it needed,' the actress asserts.

19

WILSON LOUIS

Death in a Dream

'Would you believe that I actually had a dream where I saw my cousin drown? I woke up wondering if there was a well in and around Mumbai's Kalina University campus where Peter lived,' narrates writer, director and producer Wilson Louis, admitting that after witnessing his body being fished out of a well in the dream, he promptly called his uncle the next morning to enquire about his cousin's well-being. He felt relieved upon hearing that Peter was fast asleep in his room.

However, shortly after that incident, Wilson learnt that another cousin, who resided in Mangalore, had drowned in a well. 'I hadn't known Ambrose well, but I immediately noticed his striking resemblance to Peter,' he informs, sending a chill down the spine.

At times, Wilson had dreams, while on other occasions, he had hallucinations when wide awake. These occurrences continued and intensified, particularly in 2020–21 during the Covid-19 pandemic. The film-maker found himself seeing many loved ones getting injured or dying in crashes, falls and accidents. These vivid dreams even intruded into his everyday life, frightening him profoundly.

One particular evening, after the lockdown, he had accompanied a few friends to a regular watering hole for drinks. They were waiting outside for a friend to join them when Wilson had one of his unsettling 'episodes' and saw Rahul take a really bad fall from a train. Chilled to the bone, he shared the distressing vision with his friends, who assured him that Rahul was definitely not taking the local train. Wilson felt slightly relieved until his buddy arrived, and to everyone's shock, he was bleeding profusely. 'Rahul had fallen not from a train, but from a crowded bus while attempting to get off,' he shares.

The film-maker goes on to recall how he had met Saurab Narang at the Maya Digital Studio in Mumbai. Saurab had directed the horror film *Vaastu Shastra* (2004) for Ram Gopal Varma and the two had formed a bond after a mix-up over tapes brought them together at the studio. However, after that, they lost touch for a couple of years. 'Then, one night, in November 2009, I dreamt of Saurab,' informs Wilson.

Call it coincidence or premonition, but a couple of days after that dream, he bumped into Saurab at a mall. 'He was with his wife and son. When I asked him how he was doing, Saurab told me excitedly that he was making a film for UTV and would be going to Pune soon,' Wilson narrates.

The film, however, did not see the light of day. Soon after, Saurab was diagnosed with stomach cancer. The film-maker fought valiantly, even flying off to Sri Lanka to consult an Ayurvedic specialist who was attending to the then President Mahinda Rajapaksa. But his cancer was at an advanced stage and Saurab Narang passed away in Colombo on 26 June 2010, barely eight months after Wilson's dream and their last meeting.

While working on the fantasy adventure *Jajantaram Mamantaram* (2003) at the Maya Digital Studio, Wilson had another dream in which his boss, visual effects supervisor Biju Dhanapalan, was bitten by a dog. 'The next morning, Biju limped into the office. When I asked him what had happened, he smiled sheepishly and confided that he had heard some puppies crying in the trash and had gone to investigate. Suddenly, their mother had appeared and thinking he was taking her babies away, had pounced on him and bitten his leg,' he recounts.

Wilson has been associated with several projects as a visual effects producer, including Aamir Khan's *Ghulam* (1998), *Earth* (1999) and *Mangal Pandey: The Rising* (2005), John Abraham's *Jism* (2003) and *Saaya* (2003) and Hrithik Roshan's *Koi... Mil Gaya* (2003). He has also directed and released three feature films—*Ho Sakta Hai!* (2004), *Mallika* (2010) and *Kaalo* (2010), all horror thrillers.

His fourth directorial, a short film, *Holding Back* (2015), revolves around a young man who is ailing and passes away on a train to Chennai. Throughout the rest of the journey, his mother holds back her tears and pretends he is alive and seriously ill to avoid bureaucratic red-tape and the endless wait to claim his body. The poster depicting her sitting on a bench at the railway station with her dead son's head lolling on her shoulder as she waits for their pick-up to arrive is heart-wrenching.

'I had heard Shiv Kumar's tragic story from his mom, whom I met in Panvel, Navi Mumbai, while she was visiting his sister. It deeply touched my heart and I made a promise to her that if I ever became a director, I would make a film about Shiv,' reveals Wilson.

However, as the years flew by, he became increasingly busy with other projects, gradually forgetting about the story that had once moved him to tears. Then, during a lull, when he was not receiving offers to his liking and wondering what his next move should be, a serendipitous moment occurred. One day, Wilson opened a cupboard and, to his surprise, Shiv Kumar's photograph fell out.

'I don't know if it was merely a coincidence or a poignant reminder of the promise which I had made to take his story to the screen. Without wasting a second, I called his sister asking for permission to film it. I had no money, but by a strange stroke of luck, I connected with Sheila Sandhu, a woman who lived in Malaysia, who was willing to invest in this story. *Holding Back* remains one of my best works to date,' he says emotionally.

In early 2021, during the country-wide lockdown, Wilson experienced a peculiar dream involving an acquaintance's mother. He had previously met Ashok Diwan on a project, but they hadn't been in touch for about eight to nine months. In the dream, Ashok's mother, who would occasionally invite Wilson over for a meal, entreated him to save her *mangalsutra* (necklace worn by married Hindu women). Bemused, he called up Ashok and shared what he had seen. To his shock, Ashok burst into tears and revealed that his mother had passed away two years ago, and tragically, his father had also died a year back.

'Since then, I have been embroiled in a legal dispute with my younger brother over property matters. Finally, everything has been sorted out and divided, except for our mother's gold mangalsutra. We had planned to sell it, but after hearing from you, I promise to hold on to this piece of jewellery given its sentimental value for my mother,' Ashok vowed.

Interestingly, Wilson claims he had a premonition about the Covid-19 pandemic, long before it became a reality. In January–February 2019, he was to leave for Pune to prepare for a film revolving around a teacher who travels thirteen kilometres every day to teach a single student. Before leaving, he drove to his office, packed up all his equipment, books, tapes and lugged them home. When his wife protested, asking why he wanted to turn their home into a godown when he had a big office, he told her to bear with him for a few days and left for Pune.

He was staying with a friend when the first Coronavirus case was detected in Pune. Five days later, soon after he returned to Mumbai, the lockdown was announced. 'There was no way I could have gone to the office, but since I had all my stuff at home, my work was not interrupted,' he exults.

The dreams have been plaguing Wilson for years now and at times they can be terrifying. Struggling in Mumbai, he had been staying with his aunt in Kalina for a while, before moving to a room in a chawl three buildings away. Since he was not used to sleeping on the floor, he bought a second-hand sofa from his aunt's neighbours. 'But not for a single night did I sleep well on it. I had really scary dreams of lying in a coffin, covered with wet soil, ants crawling all over my body. Petrified, I returned the sofa to the original owners, who then confided that it had been their grandmother's bed. She passed away there three months ago,' he informs.

Between 1994 and 2001, Wilson shifted houses fourteen times. One of the rentals was a one-room flat in a MHADA row house in Andheri. 'I moved out of the place in just four months because it gave me the chills. I blamed it on the dampness of the flat, but one day, on the news, I saw that they had dug out twenty-one human skeletons and bags of human bones from under that row house which apparently had been built over a dumping ground,' he narrates.

The film-maker believes he is cursed with a third eye, but given his line of work in creating horror, he has now learnt to keep these dreams to himself. 'I don't like it when people simply dismiss them as a by-product of my profession,' he says, adding that over the years, he has come to realize that these dreams are not as random as he once believed. They might be trying to convey a message, ignoring which can lead to negative consequences for someone. He shares that when he was working with a production company, he had a vision of a huge hole springing up in their office. The next morning, he sounded out his fellow workers who dismissed the premonition with a laugh.

'But a week later, I arrived to find some municipal workers clustered around a large, black hole that had been discovered just below the receptionist's desk. One of them was inside, probing around with his torch,' he recalls. While his producers blamed it on a drainage problem, Wilson interpreted it as a sign of financial loss and tried to persuade his bosses to relocate from the premises. 'They chose to stay put, but after one film which bagged a National Award, none of their other films have been commercially successful,' he points out.

A similar thing happened at another production company he was working with. Wilson's office was on the eighth floor, along with two other directors. One day, a huge glass door on their floor crashed. Rattled, Wilson, who had already complained of the negative vibes in the office, begged the producer to shift to a different floor in the same building. His pleas were disregarded. 'All the Bollywood projects that the company has invested in have either tanked or hit a roadblock,' he informs.

Wilson's first film as a writer-director, *Ho Sakta Hai!* is the story of a medical student who is urgently summoned back from the US by his grandfather after his brother and sister-in-law disappear mysteriously. Back in his village, he finds that their young son is behaving strangely, refusing to talk to anyone, waking up in the middle of the night and flinging his toys around. All fingers point to Parvati, the caretaker's wife, who practises black magic.

As part of his prep, Wilson had read up on black magic. One day, during this period, he ended up with one eye turning brown and the other green. 'None of the eye specialists I went to could give me a rational explanation for why this had happened. Some attributed it to colour pigmentation, but I pointed out that I had not been in any accident. Despite all the medication, my eyes have remained that way. With time, the colours are less pronounced, but I still have to hide the disparity behind glares,' he confides. 'Maybe it was black magic,' he adds in a whisper.

When he was ten, Wilson had a recurring dream of his eyes leaking pus. But it was only years later, in 2018, that he actually got a boil on his eyelid which grew bigger by the day and soon his eyes were filled with pus. 'The doctor I consulted asked me whether I had been near a cement factory. When I admitted to shooting a film at one, the ophthalmologist told me there was the possibility of a tiny splinter flying through the air and entering the eye. That doctor helped cure my eye, but I'm still wondering how I foresaw it years before it actually occurred,' he muses.

So, does he believe in *yantra-tantra*? As a science student, Wilson believes that evil can neither be created nor destroyed, it can only be deflected with positive energy. This realization has made him turn to the Bible and the Bhagavad Gita. He is also a devout Shiv *bhakt* who believes in the power of the *rudraksh* and reads tarot cards. 'I have done seven-eight readings, and when my aura combines with the other person's, I can see either their Guardian Angel or the Dark Soul standing behind them the moment that they open the cards. The Angel is light blue while the Dark Soul is inky,' the film-maker informs, adding that he has learnt through experience never to go for a project that adds up to 444. 'It will never materialize, while 333 has always proved lucky for me.'

Kaalo, which Wilson wrote and directed, has over 80 million views on YouTube and is a big draw on Star Gold. Equally popular on OTT, it revolves around a witch who returns from the dead to prey on young girls in her quest for immortality. Mention the film and the film-maker remembers an episode of sleep paralysis, an ailment he has been suffering from since he was in the ninth standard. 'I'm unable to move or speak, and I find myself trapped in the grips of a terrifying hallucination when I'm in the twilight zone between sleeping and waking,' he explains. He recalls that one day, while shooting the film in a house in Jaisalmer, he dozed off between shots, and while asleep, found himself face-to-face with a man-monster not unlike Kaalo.

Wilson is a tall guy with a physique to match, but he could not shake off the monster who was sitting on his chest. 'With his spindly hands around my neck, he was slowly trying to squeeze the life out of me. Then, just when I thought the end was near, the entity rolled off me, hopping across to the next room. As I lay there inertly, he dismantled the ceiling fan, left it on the floor and lumbered out,' he rewinds.

At that precise moment, Wilson came out of the paralytic state. Trying to convince himself that the whole thing had been nothing more than a hallucination, he looked towards the next room. 'The fan was lying on the floor, dismantled. No one had entered the room apart from the monster in my dream,' he concludes.

These incidents have made the film-maker take his dreams very seriously, more so after a close encounter with evil during the shoot of *Ghat: The Hill Station* (2007) in Lonavala and Khandala. One day, when they were shooting outdoors, he was asked during a media interaction if he was only going to make horror films or planned to experiment with other genres too. 'I might not always do horror,' Wilson began, but before he could complete the sentence, he started coughing. And didn't stop for the next three days.

He had taken the security guard of his building along with him because the man wanted to work with a film unit. Noticing Wilson coughing, the guard rushed across. 'But then, he just stood there silently, staring fixedly at me for ten minutes, before unexpectedly fainting,' he remembers.

They packed up early that day and returned to the villa where they were staying. The villa had a reputation for being haunted. It is said that in pre-Independence India, British officers used to torture Indian soldiers there. Their spirits were supposed to haunt the place. While Wilson did not have any other worldly encounters there, on the way home to Mumbai, the car behind him, carrying the film's costume designer and a few other production guys, swerved when the driver suddenly let go of the steering wheel while driving down the Ghat. 'The car was going down the ravine, but fortunately, a tree broke its fall, and no lives were lost,' recounts the film-maker.

And what happened to the security guard? 'He was very ill for a couple of days. While we were in Khandala, I took him to a Muslim Baba on the suggestion of the locals, who believed he had been possessed by a spirit. Then, on our return to Mumbai, I took him to a doctor and got him treated. He recovered, but disappeared soon after. I haven't seen him since,' admits Wilson.

He has gone back to making horror films and shows with subliminal messages. 'I believe that good and evil coexist. It's like when I am reading tarot cards, if I pull out one negative card, I also pull out a divine, free will card, which if implemented, can alter your destiny,' he signs off.

20

ESHA DEOL

Terror in the Hotel

Sangeeth Sivan, the director of the romantic thriller *Chura Liyaa Hai Tumne* (2003), drew inspiration from *Charade* (1963). The film revolves around a bank heist, a missing gold coin, a deceased uncle, his frazzled niece, con partners, an Indian Embassy officer and a mysterious Romeo. Amidst all these dizzying twists and turns is a ghost story that even its director doesn't know about.

Esha Deol, the leading lady opposite debutant Zayed Khan, shares a chilling incident that occurred during a shoot in Kerala. 'All of us were staying at this nice hotel. No, it did not have a reputation of being haunted. One morning, some bleary-eyed and terrified technicians, who had been up all night, complained that they had sensed a presence in their rooms, which had really spooked them. One of them even confided that the ghost had attacked her and attempted to strangle her. While I didn't experience anything strange, there were several others who came forward with similar complaints. Like everyone else, I got the jitters too. At their insistence, everyone was relocated to another hotel,' the actress recalls.

Four years later, Esha went on to feature in Ram Gopal Varma's romantic horror-thriller *Darling* (2007). She appeared alongside Zayed's cousin, Fardeen Khan, who plays Aditya Soman. Soman is flitting between his conservative wife, Ashwini, enacted by Isha Koppikar, and his wild secretary, Geeta. All hell breaks loose when Geeta suddenly announces that she is pregnant and reacts violently to Aditya's suggestion of an abortion. In the scuffle that follows, he pushes her. She accidentally hits her head, and the impact kills her. She, however, returns as a vengeful ghost, visible only to Aditya at first, and eventually claiming her revenge by possessing his wife's body.

When asked if she believes in ghosts, Esha, who plays the role of the ghost Geeta, responds, 'I believe in God, in positive energy and divine power, in being spiritual. Since I was a child, I have recited the Hanuman Chalisa every day and I continue to do so.'

21

SANGEETH SIVAN

Hisss... Beware of Snakes

Horror is not an unfamiliar genre for Sangeeth Sivan who, inspired by a Thai film *Shutter* (2004), directed the Hindi film *Click* (2010). It centers around a photographer haunted by a dark secret—a rape victim he had loved but failed to protect—who avenges herself by making the perpetrators of the crime stab themselves fatally in the same way that she had ended her life. While *Click* didn't give Sangeeth reason to fret and fear in real life, the Malayalam supernatural thriller, *E* (2017), which he produced, brought the terrors he was recreating home to him.

As a child, Sangeeth often visited the Mannarasala Sree Nagaraja temple near Alleppey in Kerala with his family. The temple is permeated with the presence of snakes—in the hangings, the idols and even the creepers lining the paths. 'If you are lucky, you might come across a few live snakes. I have seen two myself,' admits the film-maker.

Legend has it that the first priestess gave birth to a five-headed snake, which guards the temple even today. Another story about the temple's origin sounds more credible. 'There was a huge fire in which many of the snakes were badly burnt. The lady of the house took care of them, treated their burns, and the Nagaraja (King of Snakes) appeared before her, instructing her to build a temple, granting her the right to perform puja. So, Mannarasala can literally be translated as "the hot sand that cooled down". It is also said that there is a cellar within the temple where live snakes still reside and are fed milk by the priestess at night,' informs Sangeeth.

The temple is known for a special turmeric powder that is supposed to cure several rare diseases, including leprosy, attracting numerous devotees. Women unable to conceive also seek the blessings of the Nagaraja, who has the form of Vishnu and the spirit of Shiva.

'My father, who was a photographer, was shooting a documentary on the temples of Kerala. I would often accompany him to the locations where he was shooting. That was the first time I visited the Mannarasala temple. It is a beautiful place but creepy. Even the creepers look like snakes. The deity inside is very powerful,' asserts Sangeeth.

Another temple, Chottanikara Bhagavathy, dedicated to the Goddess Bhagavathi, is where those believed to be possessed are brought. The producer and director recalls seeing horrific scenes of exorcism there. 'Women with their hair open and swaying as if in a trance… Men and women with blood pouring down their faces screaming in agony or maybe fury… I still wonder if they were really possessed or suffering from some kind of mental illness,' he muses.

E, directed by Sangeeth's assistant Kukku Surendran, dredged up these early memories while addressing many superstitious beliefs still prevalent in God's Own Country.

The film revolves around four friends, one of whom is making a documentary on Alzheimer's disease. He visits his elderly teacher, Malathi—Gauthami in a comeback appearance—who is presumed to be suffering from the dreaded disease, which chips away at memories. 'But after arriving at the temple, they witness some strange paranormal activities and come upon Malathi trying to kill her own daughter, Athira,' the film-maker narrates.

After some research, the boys, along with Athira, discover that Malathi is possessed by the spirit of a man named Bhargavan, who, thirty years ago, in his quest for immortality, had killed two girls. He was getting ready to sacrifice a third, Athira, when Malathi caught up with him and killed him. But Bhargavan's spirit entered Malathi's body, using her to avenge his death and complete his quest. 'The only way to rid her of his evil *saaya* (shadow) is to find his bones, which she had buried deep in the forest and destroy them in a fire before the next full moon,' Sangeeth continues.

The screenplay, which had a lot of twists and turns, took him deep into the dark world of black magic and temple rituals. Perhaps the subject was playing on his mind because one afternoon, Sangeeth had a disturbing dream in which he found himself back in the Mannarasala Temple. 'While walking around, I was confronted by a snake. It was looking at me in a way that turned my blood cold as realization dawned that I had not expressed my gratitude for a boon granted. I turned towards the house where we were living with a feeling of dread. Reaching it, I discovered my son was stretched out on the bed, cold to my touch. For a minute, I feared the worst, but then realized that his heart was still beating,' he shivers, remembering the nightmare.

Sangeeth woke up from his siesta bathed in sweat. He hollered for his wife who rushed over, and after hearing about his dream, assured him that their son was fine. 'But it was only after I spoke to Shantanu, who was working in Mumbai, and heard the exasperated surprise in his voice when I repeatedly asked him if he was okay, that I could finally convince myself that what I had just seen was only a dream and not a premonition,' he recounts.

The film-maker warns that when making vows before a deity like the Nagaraja, one should always express one's gratitude when they are fulfilled. If you forget, chances are that you could be punished.

During the making of the film, something strange happened when they were shooting the ritual that awakens the spirit. 'Every time we got ready for a shot, a gust of wind would come out of nowhere and blow out the fire. After three failed attempts, the unit was beginning to get a little unnerved. I decided not to rush things and just wait for nature to settle down. Only after it gave us permission to proceed, did we go in for take,' shares Sangeeth, who has never encountered spirits in real life but does not completely negate their presence.

22

ABHISHEK KAPOOR

A Story of Miracles

Abhishek Kapoor believes that shooting a film like *Kedarnath* (2018) was made possible only because a higher power was looking out for him.

The tragic romantic drama, featuring the late Sushant Singh Rajput and debutante Sara Ali Khan, depicts a lesson in communal harmony. The film's conclusion showcases an unimaginable disaster caused by an overflowing lake in the higher reaches of the Himalayas, combined with a cloudburst, resulting in a devastating mudslide that washes away homes and people in the village below, while miraculously sparing the Kedarnath temple.

While on a recce, the writer–film-maker, who was inspired by the headline-grabbing floods in Uttarakhand in 2013, witnessed the real-scale devastation caused by natural calamities. He was aghast to see that roads had been wiped out by a recent landslide, and as he struggled to navigate the difficult terrain and inaccessible areas on his way to the shrine, Abhishek wondered if there would be any devotees at the temple.

To his surprise, he found a long queue of devotees waiting for *darshan*, of which many were poverty-stricken tribals from neighboring villages. They had trekked for days, even weeks, to reach the temple. 'I went with an open and receptive mind, seeking answers from the Supreme Being, and my first feeling on seeing the temple was that of coming home. Looking around, I felt the positive vibrations the devotees carried in their minds and hearts. While many would think twice about going to Kedarnath given how arduous the journey can be, these people have an unquestioning *aastha* (belief) and surrender to the Supreme Being with humility. That strengthened my conviction that this story needs to be told. The film was based on my personal *yatra* (journey),' informs Abhishek.

However, despite his unwavering commitment and deep sense of responsibility to the project that went beyond mere box-office success and profits, it wasn't easy ferrying a huge crew and extensive equipment to areas that are off-limits for about half the year. Even during periods when these places are accessible to locals, tourists and pilgrims, they can quickly become cutoff due to the changing weather conditions.

'One night, when the weather turned bad, I wondered how we would reach the shrine when I suddenly found a sponsor running sorties to ferry my crew of 150 people, heavy cranes, cameras and other gear up and down in the chopper, making it possible for us to get the shoot done within the deadline,' he marvels.

Something else happened that might sound like it's *filmi* (straight out of a movie), but Abhishek insists that it actually happened. 'We needed some drone shots to capture the vastness of the landscape and trace the path of the river.

Although drones were available locally, the challenge was to find skilled operators. With just two days left for the shoot, I was wondering what to do, when someone recommended a couple of drone operators in Iceland,' he recalls.

Without a moment's hesitation, the film-maker called one of the operators and urgently explained that he required their expertise at a remote place in India within the next forty-eight hours. To his surprise, the man calmly enquired about the logistics of reaching the destination if they left right away. 'I told him to fly to Delhi, take a car and drive ten hours straight, then trek up the mountains for another ten to twelve hours and they would arrive here,' Abhishek narrates.

He wasn't expecting them to make the long journey. But true to their commitment, the operators set off soon after the conversation. Unfortunately, their drones were confiscated in Delhi due to lacking certain licenses. Undeterred by the setback, they decided to leave their valuable equipment in the national capital and took a car to Uttarakhand.

'They arranged a new set of drones before setting out for Kedarnath. I was standing next to the temple, when I saw the two operators with an impressive array of gear walking towards me. "We're here, sir. Where do we go now?" they asked, after the initial introductions. It was precisely the hour I wanted to capture, and all thanks to them, I managed to get breathtaking, sweeping, top-angle shots and picture-perfect images,' Abhishek concludes his remarkable tale, insisting that it was an inexplicable, supernatural connection that brought those two drone operators to him from halfway across the world.

For the film-maker, this yatra held a deeply personal significance beyond being a mere physical or cinematic journey; it was also an inner pilgrimage.

'When you reach the temple, it's best to be honest and ask the Supreme Being for forgiveness for all the wrongs that you have done. Then, as you turn away from the shrine, you leave all your dilemmas and problems there, telling Him they are his to handle now. This takes a huge load off your shoulders and gives you the confidence that He will see you through. That's exactly what happened with me,' Abhishek signs off.

23

TANVEER BOOKWALA

Curtain Call

Tanveer Bookwala describes himself as a Bollywood junkie and a passionate foodie, with a deep obsession for comic books. He is also an author, screenwriter and film-maker, who was the Chief Creative Officer of Ekta Kapoor's Balaji Telefilms and now has his own boutique entertainment company, Ding.

Tanveer co-produced the laugh riot *Kyaa Kool Hain Hum 3* (2016), was the creative producer on *Azhar* (2016), the biopic of India's former cricket captain Mohammed Azharuddin, and Tiger Shroff's fantasy-adventure, *A Flying Jatt* (2016).

He has even produced several television series, such as *The Great Indian Dysfunctional Family* (2018), *Rashbhari* (2019) and *Asur: Welcome to Your Dark Side* (2020). He also co-scripted the erotic horror, *Ragini MMS 2* (2014), with Suhani Kanwar.

While nothing eerie happened when writing the script for a horror movie, there is an incident that still gives him the chills, even though it happened almost twenty years ago. 'My parents are separated, so I spent a large part of my childhood in my grandmother's house on Mumbai's Pali

Hill. We weren't particularly close, but I was always there for her, even when she was old, ailing and unable to recognize anyone,' Tanveer says.

When his grandmother passed away in her eighties, Tanveer's mother was with her during her final moments. 'I was at our family house in Bandra Reclamation at the time of her passing. Her death was peaceful, and despite her absence, I would frequently go to the now-empty house that had always been my home,' he shares.

One day, Tanveer decided to visit the house with his then girlfriend. They entered through the main door, walked down the passageway, turned left and stepped into a room. Tanveer excitedly showed off his new phone, explaining how it could capture pictures. The phone was pointing towards the curtain which separated the room from the passage. The curtain was almost full-length and stopped a foot before it touched the ground.

'Look how cool it is, you can…' Tanveer's words trailed off as he saw something unexpected on his phone screen. 'They looked like a child's feet and were clearly visible under the curtain. I saw them come down the passage, stop and turn till the person stood facing us with the curtain separating us,' he narrates.

Stunned, for a moment Tanveer found himself speechless. Turning to his girlfriend, he asked 'Did you just see…' She completed the sentence before he could, her eyes wide with fear, 'Child's feet.'

Her words confirmed that it wasn't an illusion or a hallucination. Trembling, Tanveer gathered courage, got to his feet and yanked the curtain aside. As he had suspected, there was no one there. 'We didn't wait another moment and ran out of the house as fast as we could,' he admits.

When asked if his grandmother had tiny feet, Tanveer thinks for a while, and replies, 'No...not really.'

Who was that mysterious figure that had taken that curtain call?

24

PRAVEEN MORCHHALE & JOHN BREAKMAS KERKETTA

Candle in the Wind

Produced and directed by National Award-winner Praveen Morchhale, *Barefoot To Goa* (2015) is an internationally acclaimed film, centered around two school-going children who stumble upon unread and unopened letters from their grandmother. Through the letters, they learn that she needs urgent medical help, and hence, resolve to go to Goa by train and bring her back to Mumbai for treatment. But in their hurry to leave, fearing their parents will get to know about their plans and stop them, they forget their tickets at home. Discovering this, the frightened duo gets off at the next station and proceeds on foot, only to reach Goa and find their grandmother's house empty, because she is at the station waiting to board a train to Mumbai. Achingly poignant, viewers will remember the film for its simple message, true-to-life performances and '*Naina do nyare*', a song that marked Yesudas' return to Hindi cinema after twenty years. However, its DoP, John Breakmas Kerketta, remembers the film for one dark night of terror.

'This happened back in 2012–13. Upon reaching Goa, my assistant, Damien Kullu, and I had checked into a hotel that was a short distance away from the one where the rest of the team was staying. That evening, we set out for Morjim to catch up with the others before we started shooting the next morning,' recounts John.

He recalls that it was a chilly winter night, and they were riding a rented Kinetic Honda scooter with him at the wheel and Damien sitting behind. Since they were new to Goa, the roads were unfamiliar and they had to keep stopping to ask for directions. Every time they stepped out of the little pockets of civilization, it would get darker and the roads would grow more deserted. There were paddy fields on both sides, and the only sounds they could hear were the rhythmic chirping of crickets and the occasional croaking of frogs.

'It had just rained, and the strong, chilling wind made an eerie whooshing sound,' reminisces John. The dense fog enveloped the surroundings, reducing visibility to a mere four to five metres, even with the scooter's headlamp on. To make matters worse, the network signal on their phones was weak and erratic, and the phone batteries were dying.

'Without GPS, we were lost, and it felt as if we were travelling through space. After riding in the dark for what seemed like forever, we prayed that we come across a hotel, where we could hole up for the night, or at least a petrol pump, so we could refuel our fast-emptying tank. We finally spotted a faint glimmer of lights through the fog,' he recalls.

It was way past midnight by then and John was relieved to see that the source of the light was a couple of candles lit around a cluster of idols beneath a tree. Their flames were wavering, but they stayed put despite the gusty wind. 'The candles were half burnt, pointing to the fact that there were people living close by. I looked around, but I couldn't spot any houses, only fields for miles. Peering closer, I inspected the deities. I had expected to see idols of Mother Mary, Jesus or even Hanuman, but these Gods were unrecognizable,' he recalls.

With a shiver, he got back on his scooter and decided to ride till the end of the lane in the hope that they would come across someone. But they only reached a dead end. So, he zoomed off in the opposite direction, but again, there were no signs of life, just an inexplicable sense of dread. Spooked, John decided to get back on the road.

He had gone a short distance when suddenly, he braked to a stop. 'I thought I had seen someone walking, but since my attention had been on the road, I had passed the person. I couldn't have gone further than fifty feet,' John narrates.

What made the situation even scarier was that at one point, he felt the scooter being pulled from behind. For a moment, he thought it was Damien playing a prank, but when John asked him, his assistant seemed genuinely perplexed and insisted he had not done anything of that sort. 'Suddenly, the scooter started groaning, as if it had fallen into a pit or got stuck in the mud, which was strange because the road was completely smooth and devoid of mud or potholes. Thank God, Damien and I were together that night. I dread to think what might have happened had I been alone,' John shudders.

They drove around aimlessly till around 4 a.m. Lost and disoriented, they were wondering if they would see the light of day when suddenly, a couple of cops appeared out of nowhere and stopped them. 'There had been a terror attack not too long ago and they were suspicious of two men riding around in the dark. We showed them our identity cards and told them we were there to shoot a film. They finally believed us and directed us to a hotel,' says John.

It was 5 a.m. by the time they reached their rooms. Their phones had died and neither of them was carrying a charger. 'We crashed immediately and didn't wake up till past noon,' he adds.

Praveen Morchhale admits that in their hotel the rest of the team was wondering where John and Damien were. They had waited all night for them, but the two seemed to have disappeared. 'We couldn't even reach them on the phone and we were worried sick. We cancelled the next morning's shoot and started making enquiries. They finally turned up in the afternoon, and only after they had assured us that they were fine did we start filming,' informs the film-maker.

There was another scary night during the shoot of the same film when the whole unit turned up at Manas Inn in Sawantwadi. Praveen had booked the place online, liking the look of the huge white haveli in the ads. But when they arrived at the resort, they discovered it was in the middle of a jungle despite being just two kilometres away from the city. The haveli looked dark and unkempt, exuding an eerie silence akin to a tomb.

'The ground outside was littered with dried leaves that no one had bothered to rake for an eternity. The gate was closed, and there was no security guard in sight. We kept hollering for someone to let us in, but our pleas went unheard,' he reminisces.

Eventually, one of the boys scaled the *Om Shanti Om*-like gate and entered the premises. He knocked on the door and shouted for almost ten minutes before an elderly man, wrapped in a blanket to ward off the winter chill, emerged, holding a lantern in his hand. It was a scene straight out of a horror film. He opened the gate and the rest of the team straggled in. It was quite late by then and the crew was starving. But when they inquired about dinner, the old security guard, rather brusquely, said, '*Yahan khana wana nahin milega.*' (You won't get any food here).

As they entered the haveli, they noticed that though there was a dustbin on every floor, the trash hadn't been emptied in months. None of the rooms looked occupied and there were no guests around. The floor was filthy, the rooms festooned with cobwebs and streaked with dust. The dim yellow lights accentuated the sense of doom.

'The state of the bathrooms was equally dismal. The washbasins were chipped and bore unsightly stains, while the taps were rusty from disuse. When we turned them on, some of them came off in our hands. The ones that remained standing unleashed a ghastly stream of reddish-brown water, which in the dim light, looked exactly like blood.' Praveen shudders.

There was no staff around, and the corridors loomed with unsettling shadows. Praveen recalls how the girls in the unit were so frightened that they chose to stay together in his room. 'We stayed up all night, occasionally darting apprehensive glances at the huge bathtub resting on rusted crab claws in one corner of my bedroom, wondering if it would end up being our coffin. A couple of pranksters let out muffled screams from the nearby rooms, adding to our fears,' the film-maker shares.

The next morning, as sunlight bathed the surroundings, the hotel appeared a lot less menacing. The setting was picturesque, and there were some people and a few cops around as well. 'To this day, my art director and costume designer, along with my niece, remember the place as the '*bhootiya haveli*' (haunted house). There is a hotel and bar there now, which is a nice stopover,' says Praveen.

John points out that it's strange how a place that had seemed welcoming with its burning candles turned out to be ghostly, while another location that appeared to be a haunted house was, in reality, quite safe.

25

AKSHAY OBEROI

Sleepless in the Graveyard

In 2014, director Akshay Akkineni made a Hindi remake of the Tamil horror film *Pizza* (2012). Prepping for it turned out to be a spine-chilling experience for the film's lead actor, Akshay Oberoi, who at the time didn't believe in spirits, and is still confused about whether they exist.

In the film, Akshay's character, Kunal Malkholkar, finds himself locked in a bungalow where he goes to deliver a pizza. There are about half-a-dozen ghosts in the house, one of whom could be his pregnant wife. Kunal struggles to leave the house, even as slices of pizza keep disappearing and the horrors pile up.

In order to prepare for the role, the actor decided to spend a night at the cemetery next to Mumbai's SNDT College.

'Since I was not a recognizable face back then, I walked down the relatively empty street around 1 a.m., reached the graveyard and lay down on one of the benches there. I swear I heard all kinds of strange noises that kept me up long into the night,' Akshay recounts.

At one point, he fell asleep but was awakened by a bright light flashing on his eyes. 'I awoke with a jolt, only to find that it was pitch dark and eerily silent, with not a soul in sight. This happened a few more times. I don't know if it was my mind playing tricks or if I was experiencing some strange paranormal activity. I must admit that night really spooked me,' the actor recounts.

During the making of *Pizza*, however, Akshay did not experience anything eerie, even though many in the unit claimed that Shanaya Bungalow in Madh Island, where they shot most of the film, was a haunted house. 'Several unit members swore that they had seen an apparition in the huge lawn behind the bungalow. We were working long hours for almost thirty nights at a stretch. So, most of us were sleep deprived and exhausted. A tired mind can play tricks on you. That could be a logical explanation for the 'sightings' because I didn't see or feel anything out of the ordinary,' he recollects, admitting that while the film's director Akshay Akkineni and DoP Jaya Krishna Gummadi believe in spirits, something like what he experienced in the graveyard has never happened to him again. 'Even to this day, I wonder if there was anyone in the cemetery that night.'

His co-star Dipannita Sharma also says she did not feel any paranormal presence while filming. 'Of course, I made sure that I was never alone in any part of the house,' she chuckles, adding that she was the scare factor on that set. 'Since I play a ghost and Arunoday Singh plays my ghost hubby, every time we stepped out of our respective vanity vans in full make-up, people were spooked. One day, a biker rode into a tree after spotting us in our ghost make-up and another day, an attendant who happened to suddenly come across us spilled his tea. The wardrobe guy refused to look at our faces, so I think for them at least, the whole haunted bungalow experience came true! I, for one, thoroughly enjoyed playing the part.'

The road to Marve and Madh island is notorious as one of the most haunted places in Mumbai. Enveloped by lush greenery and flanked by mangrove forests on either side, the route appears picturesque and serene. But it has gained a sinister reputation due to the high number of automobile accidents that have occurred here.

According to local legend, on a full-moon night, the ghost of a young bride materializes suddenly in front of vehicles, causing the drivers to lose concentration, leading to fatal crashes.

The buzz is, decades ago, a woman was brutally murdered on her wedding night and her body was dumped in the mangroves. Since then, she is said to turn up in the middle of the road in full bridal finery, looking directly at the petrified driver. Reportedly, the only way to save oneself is to avoid making eye contact with her.

Cops advise motorists to avoid the stretch after dark, insisting that even if they do drive through the area, they should not stop their vehicles under any circumstances.

26

TANUJ GARG

Ragini's Haunted House

In 2011, *Ragini MMS*, apparently loosely inspired by the American found-footage film, *Paranormal Activity* (2007), changed the face of horror in Indian cinema.

It revolves around a young girl, Ragini, who embarks on a weekend getaway with her boyfriend Uday, and some of his friends. Their destination is a secluded house in the woods, away from the hustle-bustle of the city. While she believes Uday loves her, his motive for the trip is to film their intimate moments and exploit the footage for profit.

However, the situation takes an unimaginable turn. Ragini finds herself handcuffed to the bed, unable to break free. In a shocking twist, Uday fatally stabs himself in the neck. To add to the horror, their two friends go missing, and a witch makes her presence felt, as the atmosphere in the house turns ominous.

The film's shooting took place in an old, dilapidated bungalow in Dahanu. The film's co-producer, Tanuj Garg, recalls the unit expressing unease about the shoot location, telling him it exuded bad vibes. 'No one could pinpoint exactly what was wrong, but two crew members, a girl and a boy, quit. They insisted they were facing a lot of problems in their personal lives ever since they had reached Dahanu. They believed that the house was the reason. I didn't know how to react because I had never faced anything like this in my life. I still haven't and wasn't even there at the location,' shares Tanuj, who still remembers those frantic calls during the twenty-five-day shoot.

When producer Ekta Kapoor heard about this, she took it seriously. 'A *pandit* was called and a *shuddhi puja* (cleansing ritual) was performed at the Balaji office, but it did not stop the duo from walking out,' he sighs.

The house had been recommended by a local contact and since it fitted writer-director Pawan Kriplani's brief, they decided to hire it for the shoot. 'The line producer later muttered something about the locals saying it was haunted, but I really wouldn't know if there was any truth to the rumours or if he was just influenced by the general antipathy towards the house,' muses Tanuj.

The film is believed to have drawn partial inspiration from the true-life story of a nineteen-year-old girl, Deepika. She accompanied her boyfriend of five months to his friend's house on the outskirts of Delhi for a night.

Later, Deepika admitted that the moment she entered the house, she felt a sense of unease and negative energy. She had an eerie feeling that someone was watching them all night, unaware that her boyfriend's laptop was furtively recording their lovemaking. The MMS subsequently went viral.

She later shared the incident with a friend who worked with Balaji Telefilms. Intrigued by the story, the friend sounded out Ekta, who immediately expressed interest in making a film on this. To enhance the plot, Ekta decided to introduce a sub-plot involving a woman, who had been branded as a witch by the locals and killed, whose spirit had taken possession of the house. 'Back then, many tried to dissuade us from making the film, saying it would be perceived as an erotica, but the plot was carefully written to avoid sleazy elements and focus on delivering a chilling narrative. Clearly the audience loved the film and it emerged as a sleeper hit,' says Tanuj.

Ragini MMS premiered on May 13—Friday, the thirteenth. It was a star-studded midnight show. Among those who walked the 'black' carpet at the event were Amitabh and Jaya Bachchan, who came for old friend Jeetendra, along with Akshay Kumar, Sushant Singh Rajput, Ankita Lokhande, Raveena Tandon, Celina Jaitly, and the lead actors Rajkummar Rao and Kainaz Motivala. At the event, waiters were dressed as skeletons and vampires, offering 'bloody' cocktails, setting the perfect ambience for the spooky movie.

With net domestic box-office of Rs 15–20 crore, the film made a significant impact on the largely untapped horror market in India. Encouraged by its success, Ekta and Tanuj discussed the prospect of creating a sequel, *Ragini MMS 2* (2014), centered around a sleazy director and an ex-adult star. They return to the same house as the prequel to shoot a film on the hauntings.

The film featured Sunny Leone, in her second film after *Jism 2* (2012). According to her husband Daniel Weber, nothing out-of-the-ordinary happened during the shooting of the film.

Ekta and Tanuj at Balaji co-produced another film involving witches, *Ek Thi Daayan* (2013), before the sequel of

Ragini MMS was released. The film featured Huma Qureshi, Kalki Koechlin and Konkona Sen Sharma as witches. It ignited the fury of Ipsita Roy Chakraverti, a self-proclaimed witch. She approached the then President, Pranab Mukherjee. She also submitted a petition to refer the film to then chairperson of the National Commission for Women, Mamta Sharma, arguing that *Ek Thi Daayan* perpetuated the age-old practice of branding women as witches and burning them at the stake. She feared that the film's portrayal might lead to an increase in witch hunts in the remote regions of the country, exacerbating an already prevalent issue.

Tanuj believes both witches and ghosts can be extremely territorial and protective of their turf. Some of his sceptical friends returned from a tour of the Bhangarh Fort in Rajasthan with some chilling stories that had left them shaken.

A *sadhu* by the name of Guru Balu Nath is said to have lived in the vicinity of the Bhangarh Fort. According to local folklore, he allowed Maharaja Man Singh I to build the fort on the condition that it should not cast a shadow over his house. He warned that if this condition was violated, the city would perish. The king kept his word, but his descendants eventually broke the agreement, leading to the sadhu's curse falling upon Bhangarh.

Another legend revolves around Princess Ratnavati, who was being pursued by a tantric named Singhia. Well-versed in the dark arts, Singhia mixed a love potion with her perfume in a desperate bid to possess her. The princess got wise to his ploy and poured the perfume over a boulder. Enraged, Singhia cursed the once bustling town, transforming it into a ghost town.

'When my friends were in Bhangarh, they experienced a disconcerting sensation—like how Deepika and Ragini felt—that they were being watched and followed. The place made them feel quite unwelcome,' says Tanuj. 'It's as if the spirits in the fort were telling them what the witch in our film says, "This is my house and I won't leave it. If you come here, I won't let you leave." Eerie!' he concludes.

27

SACHIN KHOT

Glass Effect

Sachin Kamlakar Khot begins his narrative by making it clear that he doesn't believe in ghosts. And that is why he is not convinced that what happened in Jakarta some fifteen years ago was real.

Sachin is the director of the film *Ugly Aur Pagli* (2008), and popular television series such as *It's Complicated - Relationship Ka Naya Status* (2013–14), *Ishq Kills* (2014) and *Dharmakshetra* (2014–2015).

In 2006, he flew to Indonesia to shoot a local television show. A college in Jakarta, located next to a Chinese graveyard, was their location for two days. By the afternoon of the first day, rumours began to circulate about the presence of spirits in the vicinity.

'I was quick to dismiss them as nonsense and took a round of the property. I went alone and returned unscathed and unruffled, hoping to put the stories to rest. But some unit members were not convinced, telling me insistently, '*Nahin sir, yahan bhoot hai.*' (Sir, there really are ghosts in here). I remained unconvinced,' the film-maker reminisces.

The next day, the crew moved indoors and the fear escalated. This time Sachin's colleagues claimed to have seen something. 'I followed them down a long corridor at the end of which was a glass door. The door opened into a smaller passage with another glass door at the other end. I was told by my terrified crew that they had seen something flitting between the two doors,' he shares.

Sachin peered through the glass and could see nothing unusual. His team was not reassured. 'You are not a believer, that's why you don't see anything. Besides, you have a strong will power,' they argued, somewhat disgruntled because he was not taking them seriously.

At around 7 p.m., they were filming in a hall with tinted windows, when one of the girls screamed suddenly. Then, burying her face in her hands, she broke into terrified sobs. Sachin was flummoxed because minutes ago she had been perfectly normal. When he prodded her, the distraught girl pointed to one of the black glass windows, saying she had seen a face reflected in them.

Once again, Sachin took a round of the property and drew a blank. He believes that it was their proximity to the cemetery, and the fact that the graves were visible from the location, that rattled his cast and crew and fired their imagination.

However, locals later revealed that the college had been built atop a graveyard and such strange occurrences were quite common there. In fact, Sachin, who has been to Jakarta many times after that, asserts that locals there strongly believe in ghosts and openly speak about supernatural experiences.

What's more, some of Indonesia's biggest domestic box-office grossers, including *KKN di Desa Penari (KKN in Dancer's Village)*, *Sewu Dino (A Thousand Days)*, *Satan's Slaves* and its sequel and *Suzanna: Buried Alive* are horror films.

28

ANANTH NARAYAN MAHADEVAN

Trial by Fire

'I grew up in Thrissur in Kerala, in a traditional joint family. Our ancestral house had a large front portico and a backyard filled with coconut trees. During the day, the children had the freedom to explore the vast property, but as evening approached, we were strictly warned against venturing out, especially standing under a banyan tree,' recounts National Award-winning writer, actor and film-maker Ananth Narayan Mahadevan.

Ananth explains that the prevailing belief back then was that during the twilight hour, *yakshis* (female nature spirits) hang from trees, particularly ancient groves, and pounce on anyone standing beneath. 'The curfew hours started at 6 p.m. and extended until daybreak,' he adds.

He goes on to share another superstition associated with the night in his hometown. 'We were told that at 3 a.m. every day, the river Ganges wakes up and goes for her bath. We grew up hearing that no one should bathe before her,' he narrates. 'A priest from the Thiruvambady Sri Krishna Temple had ventured out for a dip around the time. When he had come up for air, he apparently saw an apparition sitting on the steps of the temple pond. They found him lying unconscious near the pond at dawn. After the incident, he is said to have lost his mental balance.'

Ananth has no idea whether these stories are true because fortunately for him, he has never encountered a yakshi, but they, along with a few cases of alleged possession, instilled the fear of the occult in the residents of the temple town. 'Every time I came across a banyan tree, I would shut my eyes tightly and invoke the name of Ram,' he admits. After coming to Mumbai and becoming a part of the film industry, he heard many stories of hauntings around Film City Studio and the infamous Malad-Marve Road. He learnt to harness his inner strength to protect himself from such paranormal assaults.

Ananth wrote and directed *Anamika: The Untold Story* (2008), based on Daphne Du Maurier's literary classic *Rebecca* (1938). By the time shooting for his movie was underway, the film-maker was not afraid to walk alone around the deserted wing of the Bikaner palace while the lights were being set up for a shot. 'I was told that someone had died there, after which the place was believed to be haunted and subsequently abandoned. I admit, it did feel spooky and was perfect as the haveli of Vikram Aditya Singh Sesodia, where a ghost from his past returns to haunt him and his second wife, Jia,' he reasons.

In the film's final scene, the caretaker sets fire to the house in a desperate attempt to kill Jia, only to die in the flames herself. Ananth was wondering where to stage the climax, when the man who had rented out the place to them, gave him permission to set one of the wings on fire. 'No one goes there. You are the first visitors in years. It's best that you destroy the dump before you leave,' he told the film-maker, who jokes that in this way the ghosts of this haveli were laid to rest.

On 8 February 1989, a devastating fire engulfed the sets of Sanjay Khan's television drama series, *The Sword of Tipu Sultan* (1990–1991). The presence of loose wires, huge lights and gunny bags in the walls, and the absence of ventilators and other firefighting equipment, led to sixty-two people losing their lives at Mysore's Premier Studios during a shoot. Among the injured was the film-maker himself, who spent over a year in hospital and despite seventy-two surgeries, was scarred for life.

The memory of the fire still sends shivers down Ananth's spine. He was playing the role of Diwan Pandit Purnaiya and had to report for shooting that fateful day. 'I had an early morning flight to catch and had instructed the driver to pick me up from my Wadala residence at 3.30 a.m. When he failed to turn up even at 4 a.m., I ran to the station, hopped onto a cab, drove back home to pick up my luggage and raced to the airport, making it just in time,' he recalls.

Ananth reached Bangalore (now Bengaluru) to discover that there was no car waiting for him. So, he took a cab and he finally arrived at the studio in Mysore around 6 p.m. 'The cab broke down thrice on the way.'

Inside the studio, Sanjay Khan was shooting on a village set. Observing how cramped it was, Ananth asked the film-maker why he hadn't chosen to shoot in the more spacious Film City Studio in Bombay (now Mumbai). In response, he was curtly told to check out the floor where he would be shooting the next morning. After taking a round, the exhausted actor decided to head for the apartment which would be his home for the duration of the shoot and grab an early dinner, not having eaten all day.

'I rounded up four of my co-actors and we got into a van. We had just driven out of the gate when we heard a huge explosion. Looking back, I saw the whole studio blow up in front of my eyes. Boom!' he narrates.

The next time he was inside the studio, it was pitch dark and there was a pile of charred bodies. Ananth admits he will never forget that sight and the smell as long as he lives. In retrospect, he believes that some force had been conspiring all day to keep him away from the ill-fated shoot. 'Another five minutes and I would have been history too,' he shivers.

After the fire, everyone had assumed that the television show would be canned. But six months later, Ananth was told that auditions for the show were being carried out at Sanjay Khan's bungalow. He arrived at Sanjay Plaza to find the actor-film-maker's younger brother, Akbar Khan, in charge of the proceedings, as Sanjay was still recuperating in hospital. To his shock, he also discovered that another actor had been cast in his place. 'When I protested, I was told, "Oh, we thought you had been 'left' behind in Mysore." The words still haunt me,' admits Ananth.

29

SONAL SEHGAL

The Pain Returns...

Sonal Sehgal is best remembered as John Abraham's fiancée in Nagesh Kukunoor's *Aashayein* (2010), who accompanies him to the Himalayas to drink from a waterfall that, it is believed, will cure his cancer.

Nine years after that film, Sonal made her debut as a film producer. She joined hands with a like-minded fellow student from the New York Film School, Latvian film-maker Dace Puce, to work on *Manny* (2020). While Dace directed the film, Sonal scripted the sci-fi adventure and played the role of the protagonist, Maya, a writer and closet homosexual who travels to Latvia to work on an autobiographical novel.

Soon after landing there, Maya tears a ligament in her right shoulder while lugging her baggage. She ends up becoming not only physically but also emotionally dependent on Artificial Intelligence (AI) to complete the book for her. The story unfolds through her three love interests, real, imaginary and virtual—man, woman and AI.

The Indo-Latvian team began filming in December 2019 and was progressing smoothly, thanks to a detailed two-week workshop for the multinational cast and crew before the shoot. 'On the last day of the shoot, I woke up, like Maya, with a searing pain in my right shoulder. It was in the exact same spot as hers. Neither had I lifted anything heavy nor had I slipped and fallen. Spooked, I texted Dace saying Manny had got me,' Sonal recounts with a laugh.

Fortunately, they were almost finished and the producer-actress powered through the shoot despite the inconvenience. But the mysterious pain lingered on for a week.

In retrospect, she admits that it could have been brought on by the cold. 'I am a Mumbai girl and from 30 degrees Celsius to minus 6 degrees Celsius was a shock to my system. Every time I had to step out to face the camera, our concerned director would instruct the assistants to make sure I didn't die, warning them that there was still a few days of work left and should anything happen to me, they would not get paid,' Sonal chuckles at the memory.

When questioned about how the pain could have been caused by the freezing temperature, considering she had likely acclimatized to it by the end of the month-long shoot, she responds, 'True, but if we dismiss the cold, what then caused the frozen shoulder?'

Parts of the film were shot indoors. While shooting inside a house was much cosier, it was quite eerie. 'Latvia is a beautiful country, but it is so sparsely populated that the houses are few and far between. The one where we shot was in the middle of nowhere,' Sonal reminisces.

She believes the house had a history, but the team was careful not to tell her, afraid that she would run off. 'It gave off spooky vibes,' she shudders.

The five-star hotel where they were staying had been jam-packed in November and through Christmas. But it inexplicably emptied out during New Year because of the cold. 'One morning, I went down to the dining room to find just three people having breakfast. The rows of empty tables were disconcerting. China was struggling with the first wave of Covid-19 and it had reached a few other countries by then. Perhaps that's what made the tourists pack their bags and head home. Since we were cut off from everyone, we had no idea a pandemic would soon bring the world to a standstill.' Sonal stayed in Europe till February before returning to India.

Fortunately for her, the next three months were busy with the film's post production, which took place over email and virtual meetings. However, isolated from family and friends, Sonal realized even better the interdependence between man and gadgets/AI, which is *Manny*'s theme.

Manny grew out of an online shopping spree. 'I was looking for a pair of shoes and found one I liked. I eventually decided against buying them since I wasn't sure of the size. However, I couldn't forget about the shoes, as ads popped up whenever I opened Facebook or Instagram,' she says exasperatedly, pointing out that one has to be careful not to spend too much time surfing online or get too dependent on gadgets and apps.

She gives the example of a lazy friend who was constantly rapping out instructions to Alexa, his virtual voice-based assistant. 'Then, one day, when we were chatting about a mutual friend, my friend called him a "bastard". Instantly, he was reprimanded by Alexa, who, borrowing a phrase that she had heard earlier, told him "that was not nice", leaving us both startled,' narrates Sonal.

She has since learnt a lot about AI, available to millions through gadgets like Alexa and even the handy smartphone. 'If you sleep with the phone next to you, know that it is watching you and reading your subconscious mind,' is her final warning about AI's omnipresence as it threatens to become George Orwell's Big Brother who is always there, watching!

30

PRASHEN KYAWAL

Lost!

'If you are from Maharashtra or the Konkan region, you would have heard of the *chakwa*,' says Prashen Kyawal. Elaborating on the subject, he informs that they are mischievous spirits who will not harm or pose any danger. 'If you are out in the jungle or a deserted place late at night, they may only misguide you and make you go round in circles. Their power fades in the light of the day, and then, you will eventually find your way out, returning home dazed, but otherwise unhurt,' he explains.

Prashen is the creative producer of *Rakkhosh* (Netflix, 2019), the post producer of *Chhorii* (Amazon Prime, 2021), *Kathal* (Netflix, 2023) and the action film *Kill* (releasing in 2024) which had its world premiere at the Toronto International Film Festival (TIFF). He had heard about these ghostly pranksters, but he was not particularly concerned when he embarked on a journey with his family to visit the Khandoba Temple at Jejuri, situated southeast of Pune. 'It was late, close to midnight, and the drive seemed never-ending. Suddenly, we realized that we had been passing the same village repeatedly without moving forward,' he recounts.

Scared, he stopped the car at one of the huts in the village and tentatively shouted '*Koi hai*? (Anyone there?)' Initially, no one responded, but after a while, a man stepped out of the hut. He looked at them strangely when they mentioned where they were headed. Then, he pointed them in a particular direction and muttered some instructions. 'I wasn't sure if he had shown us the right path but relaxed a while later when I realized we had reached the highway again,' admits Prashen, who to this day, relives the terror of being lost in a *bhool bhulaiya* (maze), wondering if the village they passed and the man they met were real or an illusion spun by a *chakwa*, who are known to play tricks on the mind.

Another time, he was driving home from a shoot in the Murud Janjira fort in the Raigad district of Maharashtra. Since it was late at night and all his co-passengers were fast asleep, he also started to feel drowsy. Wanting to clear his head before driving further, Prashen stopped near a small village shrouded in darkness. 'Peering out of the window, I noticed a tea stall near a covered bus stop. But since it was so late, there was no one around,' he reminisces, adding that in the light of the car's headlights, he also noticed a small temple by a peepal (sacred fig) tree. 'After that, I remember nothing. I just nodded off.'

After a while, he woke up with a start. Feeling slightly better after his nap, he started driving again. Perhaps from the sudden motion, one of the guys in the car woke up too and started looking around. Still half-asleep, he muttered, '*Hum galat jaa rahe hain*' (We are not on the right track).' Prashen was aware that this guy knew the route well, so he turned on Google Maps, which showed him that they were headed towards a forest. 'I tried to get us back on track, but we kept going round in seeing that village and that temple again and again,' he narrates.

Just when he was beginning to get seriously worried, a police jeep came out of nowhere and parked diagonally across the road, forcing them to brake to a stop. 'The officer walked up to us and asked to see our identity cards. When I told him that we were headed to Mumbai, the officer told me to follow his jeep. Thankfully, he guided us back to the highway and told me which landmarks to look for on the way,' Prashen shares, the relief evident in his voice. 'I have driven down that route many times since that day, but I never came across that village with its tea stall, bus stop and temple ever again,' he admits.

Prashen served as the creative producer on the psychological drama *Rakkhosh* (2019). Touted as India's first POV film, it is a modern adaptation of Narayan Dharap's Marathi short story, *Patient No. 302*. The film features Sanjay Mishra, Tannishtha Chatterjee, Priyanka Bose and Barun Chanda. The story unfolds from the perspective of its lead character, Birsa, a schizophrenic with a history of abuse, who is now confined in an asylum.

They wanted to shoot in an actual asylum but obtaining permission proved challenging. 'So, we settled on a deserted building on the outskirts of Nagpur. No one goes there and it is largely unused, having acquired a reputation of being haunted,' informs Prashen, who wasn't deterred by the ghost stories. 'We cleaned the place up and shot two schedules of twenty days there. It reminded me of a novel I had written as a teenager.'

His story, *Bhootacha Shodh,* revolves around a group of young children who go for a vacation to their ancestral village in the Konkan belt and launch an investigation to determine if the notorious *bhoot bangla* (haunted house) in the village is truly haunted. He refuses to reveal the suspense, but when asked whether he encountered any spirits in this haunted bungalow, Prashen laughs and says, 'No, the real terror was what we concocted on screen, growing out of a crazed mind. A "living" *rakkhosh* (monster) is always scarier than a dead one.' Touche.

31

ALISHA 'PRITI' KIRPALANI

Ctrl, Alt, Delete

Visualize this: A book about the family that brought horror to Hindi cinema, the Ramsays, with films such as *Andhera* (1975), *Darwaza* (1978), *Sannata* (1981) and *Purani Haveli* (1989), is being written. It focuses on the spirits that haunted the family. It's late at night and the story is flowing till the author—a member of the Ramsay family—reaches the paragraph where she is writing an incident about one of her seven *maamas* (maternal uncles). He has long gone from this world and the story was narrated by his widow.

'As I was recounting this potentially controversial incident, the cursor jammed. While the cursor was moving up or down freely, it would not move forward. After struggling with it on my brand-new laptop for a while, I shot a five-minute video and sent it to Tiana, my younger daughter, with a "look-what's-happening" text. And guess what, my daughter repeatedly got only those seconds of the video which did not show the jammed cursor! Bizarre!' shares Alisha 'Priti' Kirpalani, the granddaughter of film-maker Fatehchand Uttamchand Ramsay, the patriarch of the Ramsay family, who pioneered the banner that had people screaming in dark theatres across the country as ghosts ran riot on screen.

The morning after the 'cursor' incident, she spoke to her husband, Johnny, who remains guarded in his belief in the paranormal, and showed him the 'spooky' cursor. 'Realizing that it was a sign from my uncle in another world, I deleted the contentious three–four lines. And the cursor started moving freely,' she informs, the surprise still evident in Alisha's voice.

Later, someone from her uncle's family mentioned the incident, saying he hoped she hadn't put that in the book. 'I confessed that I had written about it, thinking it was not a big deal, but then, had left it out because I believed my deceased uncle had been trying to tell me not to include it,' she says, adding that it is important to respect the memories of those who are no longer with us, and also the ones they have left behind.

A weaker woman might have been scared off by this supernatural encounter while writing about the supernatural, but Alisha carried on undeterred. 'While my husband and elder daughter, Sascha, will have nothing to do with spirits, my mother and I have had ghostly sightings and dreams. Tiana, my younger one, is a chip of the old block too,' she smiles wryly.

Her third book and her first attempt at non-fiction is titled *Ghosts in Our Backyard: The Ramsays' Real-life Encounters with the Supernatural*. Published by HarperCollins Publishers India, it vividly describes certain strange occurings her family witnessed. Alisha describes it as India's first horror memoir, as an interviewer had pointed out.

'Two of my uncles, Keshu and Kiran, had already passed away by the time I started writing the book. Tulsi Maama and

Kumar Maama had seen nothing apart from imagining the ghosts in their films. But the other three uncles, Gangu, Arjun and Shyam, and my aunt, Kamla, had experienced some terrifying brushes with the paranormal, as also my mother, Maya Ramsay aka Asha Thawani, all of which went into the book. I wasn't afraid because none of it is fiction or fabricated no matter how impossible it seems,' asserts the author, who has written about a haunted palace, demonic screams and shuffling noises from a locked room. There is also a mention elsewhere of an apparition who chased after Gangu Ramsay and his wife one dark night in Mahabaleshwar.

Alisha's mother Asha was the one who came up with the idea for *Do Gaz Zameen Ke Neeche* (1972), though this has never been public knowledge till now. The script was written by Kumar Ramsay, and it was produced by her father. It was the first Hindi film offering from the 'Ramsay's horror factory', after the Sindhi film *Naqli Shaan* (1971). Directed by Tulsi Ramsay, with cinematography by brothers, Gangu and Keshu, *Do Gaz Zameeen Ke Neeche* revolves around infidelity, murder of a handicapped man and revenge. Its success at the box-office after the releases of *Shaheed-E-Azad-Bhagat Singh* (1954), *Rustom Sohrab* (1963) and *Ek Nanhi Munni Ladki Thi* (1970) led to the Ramsays adopting this untapped genre. In *Ek Nanhi Munni Ladki Thi*, a mask worn by Prithviraj Kapoor during a robbery early in the film, had sent a wave of fear coursing through the audience. This observation put F.U. Ramsay and his seven sons—Kumar, Gangu, Tulsi, Arjun, Shyam, Keshu and Kiran—on a terrifying path to unprecedented success.

While F.U. Ramsay's two daughters remained on the periphery of their professional arena, Asha is the one with the most spirit sightings. When they were living in a Juhu bungalow, the television in her mother's bedroom would start suddenly, reports Alisha. 'No one had switched it on, and the static was ear-splitting,' she recalls. Today, it's a familiar trope one sees in reel-life ghost stories but for her it's all very real because while living in the house, even her daughter had seen a woman on the stairs. 'Tiana had run to her grandmother, shivering. My mother was not surprised, having seen a shadow while watching television in the basement,' she shares.

Her uncle, Shyam Ramsay, went a step further, giving a ride to a hitchhiker one night, while driving home to Mumbai from Mahabaleshwar, where he was filming *Purana Mandir* (1984). She was dressed in white and had an unnerving presence. She sat beside him, still as a statue, her eyes lifeless and her voice gravelly. He almost screamed when his eyes fell on her feet. They were turned inwards. Was she a *dayan* (witch) or a *pretaatma* (spirit)? If this story is familiar, it's because it inspired one of Ramsays' biggest hits, *Veerana* (1988).

Alisha herself admits to being very intuitive. 'I can walk into a room full of strangers and can instantly tell which one of them is feeling low. I absorb the energy of people, both their joy and sorrow. Many times, I have reached out to strangers and offered comfort. In the same way, I have sensed when someone is ailing, even when the symptoms are not visible, and on at least two occasions, have helped avert a medical emergency by insisting on a timely check-up.'

She has also communicated messages received in her dreams from the dead to those left behind. 'Thank God, I don't get premonitions about my own family, including my ageing parents. That would drive me mad!' She shudders.

Her natural empathy extends to animals. It is quite common for dogs and cats to come running up to her. Once, when visiting a friend, Alisha wandered into the garden and came across a dog tied there. 'It was happily nuzzling me as I patted it when my friend stepped out and shrieked. Turned out that my new canine friend was a ferocious rottweiler who had bitten many people,' she laughs at the memory.

Alisha insists that she is a true Ramsay production because she was born late at night outside the Chandanwadi crematorium in Mumbai. 'A palm reader at a wedding was the first of many to point out that I have a *trishul* (trident) on my palm. The heartline forks into a trident which I was told signified that *Mata aur Shivji ka haath* (God's blessings) was on me and I would protect the man I love all my life,' she reveals.

The prediction came true. She was by her husband Johnny's side when he broke his leg while parasailing in Phuket. 'My elder daughter, Sascha, was just three months old at the time,' Alisha recalls, admitting that fall could well have been fatal.

During their twenty-fifth wedding anniversary celebrations in 2017, they had just started their Caribbean cruise, when the ship had to turn around and sail back because, out of the blue, Johnny suffered an acute attack of pancreatitis and had to be admitted urgently to the hospital. 'This time I was stuck in Miami,' narrates the author who writes under the pen name Alisha 'Priti' Kirpalani.

When asked the story behind the 'Priti' in her name, she explains that among Sindhis, a girl has to change not just her surname but also her name after marriage. 'Initially. I was excited about getting the chance to rename myself and chose Alisha, but after a while I realized it complicated things as I had been Priti for so long. So, when I started writing my books, I started using my maiden name as my middle name to retain a small part of my original identity,' she says.

32

PRAVEEN NISCHOL

Been There, Seen This!

In the 1980s, Praveen Nischol made five trips to Delhi's Mandi House over a span of just six months hoping to get the nod for a serial he wanted to make. One afternoon, the writer, producer and director went to the Doordarshan office to discuss the proposal he had submitted for telecast on the national broadcaster. Filled with optimism, he believed that his hard work and persistence would finally pay off, and his dream serial would receive the green light that day.

Unfortunately, Garg, the Doordarshan official responsible for greenlighting proposals, told him that while the idea was good for a masala Hindi film, it did not align with what they were seeking for television broadcast.

'Why don't you go back to Mumbai and make it into a film?' Garg suggested, as he turned his attention back to his files. Praveen, who had not anticipated a rejection, continued to sit there, dazed. After about five minutes, Garg, who had been lost in his work, looked up, and seeing Praveen still there, started, 'Oh you are still here!' Embarrassed, the film-maker admitted that he had no idea what to do next and so had been sitting in a daze. Upon hearing this, Garg took off his glasses, and setting his pen aside, said in a gentler tone, 'If you have time, why don't you stay and have a cup of tea with me.'

Over a cup of tea, Garg candidly told Praveen that he stood out from the other proposal makers who swung by his office every day. 'You are educated, intelligent and cultured, why don't you do something more intellectual?' Garg advised. When Praveen wondered what he had in mind, he mused. 'Something like Kabir… Tulsidas… Shrikant…'

'Shrikant' immediately sparked Praveen's interest. He had done his early schooling in Kolkata's Park English School, moving to Delhi Public School when he reached eighth standard. He went on to graduate in science from St. Stephen's College, then enrolled for a Master's degree in philosophy, but left the course midway.

Instead, he travelled to Mumbai, where his elder brother, Navin Nischol, an actor, had started shooting for his first film with his mentor, producer-director Mohan Sehgal. The film, *Sawan Bhadon* (1970), also marked the debut of another talented actress, Rekha. Praveen went on to assist Sehgal in *Woh Main Nahin* (1974), which also featured the on-screen pair of Navin Nischol and Rekha.

While in Kolkata, Praveen had become acquainted with the works of Sarat Chandra Chatterjee, the renowned Bengali litterateur, and had heard of his masterpiece *Srikanta* (*Srikanto* in Bengali). It was semi-autobiographical and showcased Sarat Chandra's literary brilliance.

Excitedly, Praveen shared his desire with Garg to adapt *Srikanta* for the screen. 'If you direct *Srikanta*, I will give you the go-ahead,' Garg told him.

When Praveen enquired about the procedure, he was told to buy the two volumes of the novel and submit them with an application. 'Where's the nearest book shop?' he prodded eagerly, and was directed to one near Regal theatre in Connaught Place. 'I'll go there right now. If I get the books, can I come back and submit the application today?' he asked, and Garg assured him that he would be in his office until 5 p.m.

And so, at 3.30 p.m., Praveen rushed out, purchased the books, found a typist to type out his application and hurried back to Mandi House. 'By 5.30 p.m., the proposal was sanctioned and the letter stamped. I returned to Mumbai with a 24-episode contract to film the first volume of *Srikanta*,' he shares.

The four-part story set in the beginning of the twentieth century details its protagonist Shrikant's interactions with four women. As a teenager, he meets Annada Didi in the forest. She is the wife of a snake-charmer, ostracized by her family and society because of her husband, whom she refuses to leave. She disappears after he dies of a snake bite, as does Indranath, the friend who had introduced Shrikant to her, but their memories remain.

Around this time, he used to go to school with a girl named Rajlakshmi. She would be all scratched and bleeding from plucking *karondas* (a kind of berry) off the thorny bushes, knowing how much Shrikant loved them. 'She would make a garland with the karondas and make him wear it. He tolerated her mischief, because he got to eat the berries,' Praveen narrates with a smile.

After a while, they had lost touch and circumstances forced Rajlakshmi to become a nautch girl. She runs into Shrikant again when he goes to Patna on a hunting expedition. Rajlakshmi recognizes him immediately, but he has no idea who she is and is rude to her. He treats her with disdain because of her profession, until he learns that she's his childhood friend and thaws. Their reunion is short-lived as Rajlakhshmi's profession drives them apart.

Before parting ways, she tells Shrikant, to whom she had lost her heart years ago, 'Don't think of me when you are happy, but when you are in trouble, remember me and I will always be there for you.' Later in life, she keeps her word. When Shrikant falls ill while travelling with a group of wandering mendicants, it is Rajlakshmi who nurses him back to health, only for him to leave her again.

Part 2 traces Shrikant's journey to Burma (now Myanmar). On a ship, he meets Abhaya, a beautiful, young woman. He is attracted to her immediately. She is travelling with Rohini, an orphan she grew up with and who is like family to her. They are on their way to Rangoon (now Yangon) to find Abhaya's husband, Rudra, who had left her soon after their marriage. Once in Burma, Shrikant and Rohini help Abhaya track down Rudra, only to discover that the rogue is married to someone else. She decides to leave him and live with Rohini, who has always been devoted to her. Shrikant returns to his native village, where he falls ill and once again, Rajlakhshmi rushes to his help.

Praveen finished Volume 1 in eighteen episodes, going against the wishes of his sponsors and surprising Doordarshan by forfeiting six episodes from the sanctioned twenty-four because he did not want to stretch the story beyond a point for commercial gains. '*Shrikant* (1987) was the first serial to be shot on a film negative. In fact, we shot it like a film, spending a lot of money picturizing two-and-a-half-minute dance sequences with Sujata Mehta, who played Rajlakshmi, to perfection. Jaidev was the music composer, and singers such as Anuradha Paudwal, Amit Kumar and Kumar Sanu lent their voices to the serial. We made absolutely no compromises,' the film-maker informs proudly.

Shrikant (1987) with Farooq Shaikh in the title role, was a hit not just in India, but was also the first Asian serial to play on BBC's Channel 1 and 2, not once, but twice, on popular demand. Encouraged by its success, Praveen also directed Abhaya's story from Volume 2 with Mrinal Dev (now Mrinal Kulkarni) playing Abhaya, Ravindra Mankani as her travelling companion Rohini and Irrfan Khan as her husband Rudra.

'This time I didn't want to go with sponsors as it was too taxing. I opted to make an independent series instead as this afforded a more flexible deadline. But I ended up sacrificing a primetime slot despite the rave reviews the first season received,' Praveen sighs. Disappointed, he chose not to film Kamallata's story, despite Doordarshan urging him to do so, and moved to making films instead.

It was during *Abhaya* that something strange happened that continues to bemuse him. Praveen narrates, 'We were shooting a scene at Mumbai's Essel Studio. Abhaya comes to the hospital where Rohini is admitted. He has been injured in a car crash while trying to save her from Rudra. Realizing how much he loves her and disappointed in the man she has married, she tells him quietly, "*Rohini, main aa gayi* (Rohini, I have come to be with you)."'

The simple words carried a wealth of meaning, because back then, it was unheard for a woman to leave her husband and move in with another man. Her decision shocked even Shrikant because it was amazingly bold for the time.

'I was standing at a distance, watching Mrinal and Ravindra rehearse the scene. And as I looked on, I had a deja-vu,' Praveen confides.

Praveen didn't know the actors from before, not even Irrfan. He had seen him in the tele-play he had done with Govind Nihalani and had immediately known he was Rudra. It was Irrfan's first major role,' says the film-maker.

It was the same with Mrinal, whom Praveen had seen in a Marathi serial, *Swami*, and had instantly decided to cast her in the complex role of Abhaya. In the same show, Ravindra played her husband, Peshwa Madhavrao. 'And I instantly knew that I wanted him to play Rohini in my *Shrikant*. In fact, I drove all the way to Pune, landing up at Ravindra's office unannounced, to tell the surprised actor, "You are my Rohini." He was quite shocked, wondering who Rohini was,' Praveen laughs, recalling the moment.

When he explained that he had come to offer the actor a leading role in his big budget show for Doordarshan, Ravindra was both touched and honoured. 'I will do whatever you want me to do,' he had told Praveen.

'During rehearsals, Mrinal and Ravindra who are such sincere actors, looked deeply in love, as they played out the scene. But strangely, I could anticipate exactly what she would say and how he would react and vice versa, long before they had even started. It was a surreal feeling, like I had seen this happen earlier, in another time. Actually, not the actors, but the characters, and since this novel is semi-autobiographical, I wondered if I had watched the real Abhaya and Rohini interact this way in another life. It may sound somewhat strange, but truth, as they say, is stranger than fiction,' muses the film-maker.

In 2007, Praveen joined hands with Ram Gopal Varma and produced three films with him—the political crime thriller *Sarkar Raj* (2008), another thriller set against the backdrop of terrorism, *Contract* (2008), and *Phoonk* (2008), revolving around revenge and black magic. One would have expected that given his earlier experience, there would be some spooky moments during *Phoonk*. But he insists that nothing out of the ordinary happened during the shoot of this horror film.

'I don't believe in ghosts. It was only that one time during *Shrikant* that I experienced this eerie sense of deja-vu. Maybe I was too close to the subject and the characters. But then again, I have always been passionately involved with all my projects and something like this has never happened before or since …' he trails off, still at a loss to explain why he felt the way he did, even after three decades.

33

VIKRAM KHAKHAR

Tell Me a Story

When producer Vikram Khakhar was in college, he, along with his friends, tried communicating with the dead a couple of times. 'It was all fun and games, so when a close friend insisted that we use our homemade Ouija board to help him trace his missing cousin, we admitted that we were no experts. But she had been gone for three to four days and our friend was desperate to find his cousin. So, eventually, we gathered around for the seance and reached out to some of his dead relatives half-heartedly,' reminisces Vikram, who has produced movies such as the Abhay Deol-starrer *One by Two* (2014), Randeep Hooda's much-appreciated *Main Aur Charles* (2015) and *Dobaara: See Your Evil* (2017) with siblings Huma Qureshi and Saqib Saleem.

To Vikram's surprise, they managed to forge a connection with a spirit they summoned. To prove it was a fluke, they called another and then a third. 'All three of them pointed to the letter 'M' among the jumble of alphabets when asked to pinpoint the missing cousin's whereabouts. It spooked me and hurriedly packing up the Ouija board, I sent my friends back home. But in a couple of days, my friend's cousin was located on the Malad highway, a far-flung suburb of Mumbai,' narrates the film-maker who, years later, went on to start a horror film factory called Weeping Grave Productions, in partnership with an affluent businessman, Harsh Punjabee. Perhaps the inspiration for that came from what happened later.

'When I was in college, I joined an events management company. We were managing a college fest, where one of the girls on campus showed a definite interest in me,' Vikram confides.

Being mutually attracted to each other, it wasn't very long before he was cozying up to her. As they grew close, she confided in him about her health issues. Vikram was immediately concerned, reassuring her that all would be well soon.

'But one day, I really freaked out. She was behaving so unnaturally that I thought she was having a seizure. Then, I heard her screaming in a voice which most definitely was not her own and realized that this was not a medical emergency but something else,' he shudders, adding that a few days later, when he spoke about the incident to one of her close friends, he was told that the girl was 'possessed'. Fact or fiction, Vikram didn't care to hang around for the answer. 'I never got in touch with her again, and the incident terrified me so much that I've been wary of getting too close to strangers since,' he admits.

The idea of a spirit taking possession of a living being is deeply entrenched in his mind after his visit to Mumbai's Mira Datar Dargah. He had heard from several people about this 'faith-healing centre' and decided to visit the dargah with his mother, Geeta, an omnist. When he saw the possessed people and their exorcism, Vikram was so shaken that he rushed back to his car, rolled up the windows and sat tight till his mother had finished making her offerings and returned to the car. Then, he drove off without even daring to look back at the dargah.

He was witness to another case of possession when he was shooting the pilot episode for a web series titled *Indian Haunted*. He had tied up with Team Pentacle, a paranormal and Ufology research organization in India, to make horror content based on real-life investigations. One episode was shot in an old, dilapidated house in the heart of Mumbai. The owner, frustrated after several redevelopment deals were revoked, approached Vikram and Team Pentacle to investigate the place. Digging deep, they learnt that the house, which stood on a large plot, had been bought by the owner's grandfather from an old lady in the early nineteenth century. The agreement was that she would live there permanently even after the sale came through. Life moved on and the lady passed away. But she held onto her side of the bargain and stayed put even after her death, never allowing any further resale. 'We found some *matkas* (pots) and random symbols which led us to assume that someone had been practicing black magic in the house,' shares Vikram.

Another episode for the series was shot in a *tabela* (cow shed) in Vasai, a distant suburb of Mumbai. 'We didn't see any ghosts there, but the place exuded really cold vibes,' the film-maker reminisces.

Vikram was planning to make a film on Chinmay Tiwari, a thirty-two-year-old psychic and paranormal investigator of Team Pentacle, who collapsed during a tour of one of Mumbai's oldest mills. His colleague, Shishir Kumar, spotted him gasping for breath even as the electromagnetic fluctuations on their devices went into an overdrive. 'We don't know the exact cause but would like to believe his condition was an outcome of a heatstroke and nothing sinister,' he relays.

That film did not materialize, but after *Main Aur Charles,* Vikram collaborated with Ishan Saksena and Sunil Shah to produce *Dobaara: See Your Evil*, written and directed by Prawaal Raman. It is the official Indian adaptation of the American horror film *Oculus* (2013). The story revolves around siblings, Natasha and Kabir Merchant, their parents, Alex and Lisa, and an antique haunted mirror that drives Lisa insane, pushes Alex into shooting her dead, then forces Kabir to gun down his father. He is locked up as a delinquent for committing patricide. After serving time, Kabir returns to the house with Natasha and tries to destroy the mirror that is at the root of all their problems, but unknowingly kills his sister. He is dragged back into confinement, leaving the ghosts of his parents and Natasha behind in the house. The story unfolds through time jumps between the present and eleven years earlier.

During the pre-release promotions, Saqib, when quizzed about whether there was a 'ghost' on the sets, recalled how during a sequence, he had to pick up a chair and hurl it at the antique mirror, breaking it. When Prawaal shouted, 'Action', he picked up the chair and hit the mirror, expecting a shower of splinters after the Herculean blow. But to his embarrassment, there was not even a scratch on the fragile sugar-glass mirror.

The art director decided that they would shoot the scene the next day, and Saqib went back to the hotel determined to do a better job when they resumed. However, he did not have to put in too much effort because this time, the mirror just fell to pieces on its own, startling everyone on the set. While some of the crew reasoned that Saqib's blow from the previous day had caused a hairline fracture in the glass not visible to the naked eye, others attributed it to the presence of ghosts and were too spooked to continue shooting. Eventually, a pandit was flown out to London from Mumbai and a puja was performed on the set, after which shooting resumed as usual.

Vikram believes that the mirror cracking broke a jinx that was creating unnecessary hurdles for them. 'And it wasn't just one mirror that splintered that day. There were two mirrors on the set and both happened to break on their own,' he reveals, still at a loss to explain the strange phenomenon. One of the mirrors is showcased in his office.

In 2010, the film-maker married Anchal Dwivedi, who acted in popular television shows like *Saat Phere: Saloni Ka Safar* (2005–09), *Godh Bharaai* (2010) and *Comedy Circus* (2007). Their twins, Athena and Viaan, were born on Valentine's Day, five years later. Once, while visiting his in-laws in Etawah, Uttar Pradesh, Vikram confides that his daughter woke up at night and started chatting with someone in the room. 'I opened my eyes and looked around. I couldn't see anyone else in the room. Chilled to the bone, I nudged my wife awake. Silently, Anchal and I observed our three-year-old daughter having a conversation with an invisible presence,' he reminisces.

After a few minutes, Vikram worked up the courage to ask his daughter who she was speaking to. Athena told him casually that nani (maternal grandmother) was there in the room with them and she had been telling her a story. 'My wife's mother had passed away before the twins were born,' he concludes quietly.

34

SHANTANU MOITRA

Guiding Light

National Award-winning composer Shantanu Moitra starts off by describing himself as a 'rational guy' and quoting American writer-scientist Isaac Asimov, who famously said that everything in this universe is governed by physics. When his scientific doctrine was challenged by opponents, who questioned how physics could explain the occult and events out of the ordinary, Asimov argued that man still didn't know all that there was to know about physics. What we do know, he pointed out, is science; what is currently beyond the realms of our understanding is subject to speculation till a torch shines light on it.

With this preamble, Shantanu takes a trip down memory lane to Roopkund, located high up in the Himalayas, in the Indian state of Uttarakhand. An avid mountaineer, he was in his second year of college then, and since their base camp was only a six to seven-hour trek from this glacial lake which he had heard so much about, Shantanu convinced his porter to accompany him there.

'However, the next morning, despite it being bright and sunny, Hari Singh was strangely hesitant to go trekking, telling me that the weather wasn't favourable and we should postpone our trip by twenty-four hours. But with the adrenaline rush and the daredevil nature of youth, I urged him to come along,' recounts the music director of *Hazaaron Khwaishein Aisi* (2003), *Parineeta* (2005), *Lage Raho Munna Bhai* (2006), *3 Idiots* (2009), *Naa Bangaru Talli* (2013), *Sardar Udham* (2021) and *Dunki* (2023).

The porter agreed, albeit reluctantly, on the condition that they would retrace their steps at the first hint of bad weather. The duo left early in the morning, and planned to be back by late afternoon. But sitting there, in front of the picturesque Roopkund Lake, located at a height of over 16,000 feet above sea level, near the base of two Himalayan peaks, Trisul and Nanda Ghunti, and below the ridge of the Junargali rock face to the North, the peak of Chandania Kot towering to the East, Shantanu went into an almost hypnotic trance. This dreamlike state, brought on by the rarified air, the exhaustion of a long trek and a steep climb and the majestic beauty of nature, is not uncommon to feel in the mountains. However, his Garhwali porter was fully alert and soon pointed to a black line in the far horizon, insisting a storm was approaching and they should leave immediately. Basking in the warm sunlight, Shantanu did not budge from the boulder on which he was perched. After repeating the warning a couple of times, Hari Singh simply picked up his bag and left.

Shantanu was oblivious to the fact that he was alone till the storm was almost upon him, flashes of lightning streaking through it, the wind picking up speed and beginning to rustle ominously around him. Finally, registering the danger he had consciously placed himself in, he stood up; but, by then, it had begun to drizzle. As he tried to make his way down, a few rocks loosened and rolled down, underlining that if the climb had been precarious, the descent would be treacherous in the oncoming raging storm.

'I decided that it would be prudent to move further inland. There were no Google maps to guide us then, but I remembered hearing that a sadhu lived in a cave close by, and I told myself that if I could take shelter there, I would be safe,' he recalls thinking.

To reach the cave, Shantanu had to cross a narrow pathway which dropped steeply on both sides. With nothing to hold on to, it was a free fall if you missed your step. But knowing a secure retreat waited less than two hundred metres away, he willed himself to move down the pathway and to do so cautiously. As he was crossing it, the wind started to howl around him and a white cloud enveloped him from all sides.

'It's what we call a "Whiteout" in the mountains, a mixture of cloud, snow and mist that reduces visibility to zero.' Shantanu shivers at the memory of it. His mind warned him not to go any further and he simply knelt down in supplication, the rain lashing him. 'The most horrific five minutes of my life in the face of the elemental fury seemed almost like a lifetime.'

Just when he was beginning to lose hope of leaving Roopkund alive, a beam of light pierced through the wall of white. In its wavering light, Shantanu could discern a shadowy figure in a *dhoti-kurta*. 'My first thought was that I was not going to die alone,' he remembers.

Once he figured that the man with the torch was beckoning him to follow, lighting the pathway for him, he pulled himself to his feet and tentatively took one step at a time. 'It must have taken me an hour to cross that pathway. There were moments when I didn't think I would make it. But finally, I cleared those hundred and fifty metres and could see the cave to my right,' he narrates.

With overwhelming relief, Shantanu ducked inside and saw the acetic lost in meditation. Not wanting to disturb him, he dropped his rucksack on the floor and sat down. Before he knew it, he had passed out. He was lost to the world for a good five to six hours. When he stirred awake, it was around 10 p.m. and the sadhu was cooking dinner. 'Baba shared his meal with me, then asked me how I had landed there. I recounted my horror story, telling him that I had been able to make it to his cave only because of a good Samaritan,' the composer recollects.

The storm had abated by then and the stars had come out. Looking up at them, remembering how the man had lit up the pathway for him in the blinding rain, Shantanu promised to stop by the village on the way back and try to find the stranger to thank him for saving his life.

'Did you see him?' the sadhu prodded. Shantanu shook his head, reiterating that he was probably someone from the village. This time Baba shook his head, telling him gently that he would not find his guiding light in the village. 'He doesn't live there. He doesn't live anywhere. He died seven years ago in a storm not unlike the one you have just been through. He wasn't as fortunate as you. The mountains, in particular the pathway there, is an accident-prone spot, and many have lost their lives crossing it. But now, he has started reaching out from the darkness to help those in distress, like you today, and guide them with light to safety,' the acetic told him.

The next morning, when Shantanu was crossing the pathway, it didn't look as threatening. With the sun shining, it was no more than a hop, skip and jump on a slightly dangerous path. He realized that while what he had experienced the previous afternoon could well be dismissed as a hallucination brought on by fog and fear, he was equally sure that, blinded by the storm, he would not have been able to cross the pathway without the torch of the shadowy figure showing him the way. 'There is no plausible explanation for what happened, and I have never forgotten that man, who might or might not have been alive,' he admits.

Later, Shantanu discovered, through coverage in BBC and National Geographic, that Roopkund Lake has become infamous as the 'Lake of Skeletons' after H.K. Madhwal, a forest ranger of the Nanda Devi National Park, in 1942, stumbled upon human skeletons in and around the lake. By the next decade, investigations had started into the macabre pile of bones. The British officers were worried that they were the remains of Japanese invaders till it was proved that the victims belonged to an earlier time. In the fifties, the Anthropological Survey of India conducted a study and from their head injuries concluded that the victims had been caught in a deadly hailstorm.

According to local legend, they were the bones of the king of Kanauj, his pregnant queen, their entourage and a dance troupe who had died in a blizzard while on the Nanda Devi Raj Jat Yatra that happened once every twelve years. Some believed the skeletons belonged to Indian soldiers who had tried to invade Tibet in 1841 or even Tibetan traders who had died in an epidemic or from exposure to the elements.

In 2003, a National Geographic team retrieved around thirty skeletons, some with flesh still attached to them. In 2019, following a five-year study of thirty-eight skeletons, it was surmised through radiocarbon dating and genome-wide analysis that they came from three genetically distinct groups and three different eras. Some had South Asian ancestry, one was from South-East Asia, while the remaining came from the Eastern Mediterranean, specifically present-day Greece and Crete.

The mystery of the 'Lake of Skeletons' has yet to be solved. And while scientists and anthropologists are trying to figure out how these people from different times and different parts of the world ended up dead in Roopkund, Shantanu is trying to understand what force saved him from becoming a dead man one stormy afternoon many years ago.

'Ghosts are a subject beyond my understanding, but I have been climbing mountains for a long time and have accepted that things happen there that can't be explained,' he acknowledges.

35

TANNISHTHA CHATTERJEE

Missing!

The story of *Roam Rome Mein* (2019), a psychological drama, written and directed by Tannishtha Chatterjee, who was also part of the cast, along with Nawazuddin Siddiqui, Valentina Corti, Pamela Villoresi and Urbano Barberini, was inspired by the events of a mysterious night she experienced in Venice. The actress was in the city for a film festival, and one day, took a ferry to the mainland to go sightseeing.

Warned of thieves and pickpockets, Tannishtha had decided to leave her passport behind in the hotel, only to regret it later when she went to the currency exchange shops and they refused to entertain her. Finally, she stumbled upon a small outlet, manned by a couple in their seventies, who exchanged her money so she could happily go around shopping.

As the sun went down, Tannishtha thought it wise to get some extra money exchanged and went back to the shop. It was around 6.30 p.m. and the duo was closing up, but once again, they were most obliging. As she was leaving, the actress casually asked them where she would get to sample authentic

Venetian cuisine. In answer to her query, the man in broken English quipped, 'For that you will have to come home with us.' His wife, who spoke only Italian, endorsed this with a laugh.

Even though she was surprised by the invitation from two complete strangers, she decided to take them up on the offer. Packing all the things she had bought into a suitcase she was lugging around, Tannishtha followed them to their house, where the lady rustled up a delicious meal. 'Over dinner, the conversation moved to art and artists. The gentleman pointed out that while the world raves over Michelangelo and Rembrandt, the female artists of the Renaissance period, such as court painter Sofonisba Anguissola, Bolognese portrait painter Lavinia Fontana, Milanese still-life painter Fede Galizia or even Baroque painter Artemisia Gentileschi are not as well known. He mentioned that their daughter was an architect which explained his interest in art. When I enquired about her, I was told that she had gone missing,' Tannishtha reminisces.

It was around 9.30 p.m. when the man abruptly broke off the conversation and disconnected from everything that was happening. Tannishtha remembers that he told her in a strange voice that it was time for her to leave. 'He pointed out that the last ferry to the island where I was staying left at 10 p.m. But there was something about his behaviour, which had been cordial so far, that was disconcerting. Even his wife was sitting in a way that seemed odd. I left quickly, walking straight to the ferry stand even though I had no idea where it was,' she recounts.

The next morning, Tannishtha went back to the mainland and hunted out the money exchange outlet so she could meet the old couple and thank them for their hospitality with some gifts. To her shock, however, there was no shop to be found there. Only a solid wall which the neighbours insisted had been standing there for the last twelve hundred years. She searched high and low for the duo, but there was no sign of them either.

'To this day, I don't know if they existed. My dad insists that I had had a little too much wine and was hallucinating, which he believes is not surprising given all the water around. But I had visited several other shops too that day and I remembered the faces of their owners. When I checked, those shops were all there. Only this one had disappeared, even though I had taken a picture standing across from it,' she points out, still bemused.

Tannishtha has not been able to solve this mystery to this day, but she did turn the eerie incident into a film and left it for the viewers to interpret it how they like. 'In *Roam Rome Mein* too, a girl goes missing, and we talk about Renaissance artists who have disappeared into the mists of time. It was magical how the film got made, almost as if some force was driving it,' she shares, rueing that because the schedule was suddenly pushed forward, they didn't have enough time to get permission to shoot in Venice and had to film in Rome instead.

Roam Rome Mein premiered at Busan Film Festival in South Korea on October 5, 2017, and was showcased under 'A Window on Asian Cinema'. It bagged its debutant director the Asian Film-maker of the Year Asia Star Award. It was also screened at the Mumbai Academy of Moving Image (MAMI) festival and at the International Rome Film Festival. After that the Covid-19 pandemic abruptly cut short the film's run. But Tannishtha was encouraged when she learnt that soon after its Busan premiere, London's National Gallery, in 2020, staged a blockbuster solo exhibition of Artemisia Gentileschi's art, the museum's first-ever show which was dedicated to a woman artiste.

By her Hand: Artemisia Gentileschi and Women Artists in Italy, 1500–1800 also showcased masterpieces by seventeen Italian artists to make the case for a broader view of women's participation in the Italian Renaissance. So, I feel I was partly successful in taking the mysterious couple's story and concerns forward,' the actress-film-maker smiles, pointing out that nothing as strange had happened to her before this trip to Venice, or after. 'In fact, I have never visited Venice since,' Tannishtha concludes.

36

RAJKUMMAR RAO

Stree... And a Great Fall

It's been five years since the Amar Kaushik-directed horror-comedy *Stree* (2018) opened in theatres on 31 August 2018, and with all its chills and thrills, went on to become one of the biggest hits of the year. The 'Stree', in this case, is believed to be the spirit of an angry courtesan, killed by jealous suitors on her wedding night. Since her untimely demise, the ghost has been haunting the town of Chanderi, returning every year, during a four-day festival, to stalk, entrap and emasculate men wandering alone at night as revenge for not being allowed to enjoy the long-craved joys of marital bliss.

Mysterious disappearances over the years have created a fear psychosis amongst the residents of Chanderi about the 'Stree'. They now paint the words, '*O Stree, kal aana*' (O Stree, come tomorrow), on the whitewashed walls of their homes with bat blood during the annual festival, believing the protective mantra will ward off the vengeful spirit. As fantastic as it sounds, the plot, as admitted by its writer duo, Raj Nidimoru and Krishna DK, is rooted in urban myths and folk legends.

In the 1980s, the frightened inmates of Rayalaseema village in Andhra Pradesh started painting '*O Stree, repu raa*' (O woman, come tomorrow) on the outside of their homes, after reports originated of a girl visiting every household following her untimely death. This legend has also inspired a Telugu film, *O Sthree Repu Raa* (2016).

In the 1990s, the ghost of a woman is said to have also haunted the industrial area of Peenya in Bangalore (now Bengaluru). It was said that the malevolent spirit came knocking at night, and mimicking the voices of their sisters, mothers or wives, lured men to answer the door. Those who did would be found lifeless outside their houses the next morning. In time, this viral urban legend led to the residents painting the words '*Nale ba*' (Come tomorrow) on their doors and walls to keep the ghost away. They were convinced that if the protective mantra was written for three consecutive days, the female ghost who was giving them sleepless nights would not return. Similar myths and legends have also been heard from other parts of India, including Uttarakhand. One has also heard of a similar story in Thailand.

In *Stree*, Rajkummar Rao plays Vicky, a ladies' tailor, who is grappling with not one, but two mysterious 'Strees' in the film. He has lost his heart to one, a charming stranger who appears and disappears at will, without knowing who she is, where she is from or even her name.

The actor admits that growing up, he had heard some really strange and terrifying stories of ghosts and entities from his friends. 'Some nights, we would all get together and share horror stories. Most of the ones narrated were fictional rather than factual, but as a kid, I believed them to be true,' he acknowledges.

The fascination with horror remained even when he grew older. Rajkummar informs that he was hooked on the *Zee Horror Show*, a popular weekly television series by the Ramsay Brothers, which aired between 1993 and 2001. Oran Peli's *Paranormal Activity* (2007) and James Wan's *The Conjuring* (2013), both of which have spun successful supernatural horror franchises in Hollywood, rank high in his list of favourite films.

The first part of *Paranormal Activity* revolves around a young couple, Katie and Micah, with the wife claiming to be tormented by an evil presence which has been haunting her since she was a child. The film is designed to look like a found-footage film, with Micah setting up a camera in their bedroom to record any unnatural nocturnal activity while they are asleep. Back then, Rajkummar had no idea that one day, he himself would act in an Indian found-footage horror film, *Ragini MMS* (2007).

Did the experience spook him? 'During *Ragini MMS*, mentally, I was already in a spooky zone. So, through the duration of the shoot, I was gripped by a constant fear of something ominous happening. Fortunately, it was all in the mind and nothing actually happened,' reveals the actor.

Rajkummar has also acted in another horror-comedy, *Roohi*, about possession. But that too went off smoothly.

However, something did happen during the shooting of *Stree*. The first schedule in Chanderi was uneventful. However, during the next schedule in Bhopal, an incident took place that still gives Rajkummar the shivers even though he is quick to add that he wasn't present on the scene when it happened and only heard about it from others.

'We were shooting in an old fort in Bhopal, which had a reputation of being haunted, following some incidents in the past. As a precautionary measure, we were all given certain mandates. Some dos and don'ts were specifically listed, which included not generating any kind of smoke within the premises or wearing perfume. We were also told that we should never be alone, but always move around in a group when shooting there,' Rajkummar shares.

On that particular day, it was way past midnight, and the film's DoP, Amalendu Chaudhary, wanted some changes in the lighting of the set in an attempt to create the right ambience for the scene. 'After a while, he asked for some *lubaan* (incense) to be burnt to make the atmosphere more eerie. A lighting technician, perched high on a wall, was watching the scene being set. Suddenly, a scream rang out, breaking the stillness of the night. Everyone rushed to the spot to find that the lightman, who had been sitting alone, had fallen to the ground. He was terrified and disoriented. In response to the unit's anxious "*Kya hua*?"(What happened?), he swore that someone had pushed him. This was odd, because there had been no crew near him when he had fallen,' Rajkummar recounts.

However, since the man insisted that he had been pushed deliberately, everyone started looking around for a potential miscreant whose prank had misfired. But despite searching high and low, they could not find anyone who might be responsible for the act. 'When I was told about the incident, I found it really scary,' the actor admits.

The technician was rushed to a nearby hospital. Fortunately, he had not suffered any serious injury. Still, the incident spooked the cast and crew. 'The place suddenly seemed actually eerie and we couldn't wait to leave,' says Rajkummar, who, as Vicky, will return to Chanderi over which a cloud of doom and dread is hovering again. A sequel to the 2018 film, *Stree 2*, is lining up for release on 31 August 2024. It won't be long before we hear the familiar line '*O Stree, kal aana*' once again.

ACKNOWLEDGEMENTS

This book would not have been possible without belief, faith and trust.

I believe that there is a force which goes beyond this world and occasionally manifests itself as unexplainable incidents or feelings that we come to attribute to ghosts or spirits, describe as weird and eerie and call intuition or premonition. And unlike reel life, this paranormal force is not always vengeful or fearful. It can also protect, heal, nurture and bring about miracles, make the impossible, possible.

Spooked! was born during the lockdown of Covid-19 pandemic. Tentatively, I suggested the idea to Shantanu Ray Chaudhuri, Chief Editor, Om Books International. He was in Delhi and I in Mumbai. Our minds, and our mobile phones, bridged the miles. I admit I was pleasantly surprised when he responded with an immediate, 'I want to do this book, send me a proposal.'

Within days of mailing it, we were messaging each other again, as I waited at the bank to withdraw money. We shook hands, virtually, over a deal agreed upon in less than fifteen minutes, well before I even returned home. That's faith... confidence...for you.

What's even more heartening is that my commissioning editor was there with me at every step in this *horror-fic* journey. Offering suggestions, brainstorming on the cover, even agreeing to accommodate four new chapters during the final editing and being admirably stoic when we had to drop a chapter after one person withdrew consent at the nth hour. Thank you, Shantanu. My heartfelt appreciation to my editors Tathagato Sen and Chakrika Pandey for their meticulous work and support.

This book also would not have happened had the force I mentioned above not aligned with me. The first month, in my quest for Bollywood's true paranormal encounters, I hit a dead end (again, no pun intended) many times. As the 'No, I haven't experienced anything out of the ordinary,' or 'I don't want to speak about that,' or even 'Don't make me a part of this, please,' piled up, I began to despair, wondering if the book was ever going to get completed.

But every time I was on the verge of giving up and telling Shantanu I didn't think this book would happen—we have lived through a few aborted projects—a friend, out-of-the-blue, would share a story or recommend someone who could give me one, affirming my faith that someone was looking out for me.

I would like to take this opportunity to thank Dhruv Somani. A journalist, movie buff and avid collector of Bollywood memorabilia, he put me in touch with Ranjeeta Kaur who had actually seen a djinn. Also, Alisha 'Priti' Kriplani, whose uncles, to my delight, were the same Ramsays whose *Veerana, Do Gaz Zameen Ke Neeche* and *Purana Mandir* I have grown up watching.

I found a fellow horror buff in film-maker Wilson Lewis who never questions any of life's great mysteries, no matter how impossible they may sound. His life itself would make for a fascinating film.

Also, Vikram Khakhar, with whom I collaborated on a series of tiny, terrifying tales for 100 consecutive days leading up to Halloween in 2017. Since we were still in lockdown when I started working on *Spooked!,* I couldn't visit Vikram's office, which in pre-Covid days resembled a horror film set with skulls, props and even a cracked mirror. But he was always a call away, connecting me to his director friends, Vishal Furia and Soham Shah.

This book belongs to all the friends who trusted me with their stories, made time in their busy schedules to speak to me and went through the drafts meticulously.

I also want to thank my mother-in-law, Pushpa, my husband, Pallab, and my daughter, Ranjika, for their love and support. Living with me can be nightmarish at times.

Finally, a shout-out to all those who believe in the 'others' like me... And gratitude to those who don't but still read this book.

